False

"Are you Jones?"

The person asking him the question was a girl—a young woman, actually. She appeared to be in her twenties, was tall with long black hair, and was wearing a jacket and trousers that had seen better days but were, at least, clean. She was better than the hotel they were standing in.

"Well?" she asked.

She was also wearing a gun on her hip, worn like she knew how to use it.

"If I am," he said, "are you going to shoot me?"

"Why would I shoot you?"

"I don't know," he said. "I'm just not used to seeing a girl wear a gun."

"I've got to protect myself."

"This is Saint Louis," he said, "not the Wild West."

"Believe me," she said, "there's a lot in this town I need protection from. But no, I'm not gonna shoot you."

"Then I'm Jones."

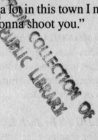

DON'T MISS THESE
ALL-ACTION WESTERN SERIES
FROM THE BERKLEY PUBLISHING GROUP

THE GUNSMITH by J. R. Roberts

Clint Adams was a legend among lawmen, outlaws, and ladies. They called him . . . the Gunsmith.

LONGARM by Tabor Evans

The popular long-running series about Deputy U.S. Marshal Custis Long—his life, his loves, his fight for justice.

SLOCUM by Jake Logan

Today's longest-running action Western. John Slocum rides a deadly trail of hot blood and cold steel.

BUSHWHACKERS by B. J. Lanagan

An action-packed series by the creators of Longarm! The rousing adventures of the most brutal gang of cutthroats ever assembled—Quantrill's Raiders.

DIAMONDBACK by Guy Brewer

Dex Yancey is Diamondback, a Southern gentleman turned con man when his brother cheats him out of the family fortune. Ladies love him. Gamblers hate him. But nobody pulls one over on Dex . . .

WILDGUN by Jack Hanson

The blazing adventures of mountain man Will Barlow—from the creators of Longarm!

TEXAS TRACKER by Tom Calhoun

J.T. Law: the most relentless—and dangerous—manhunter in all Texas. Where sheriffs and posses fail, he's the best man to bring in the most vicious outlaws—for a price.

THE GUNSMITH

393

THE COUNTERFEIT GUNSMITH

J. R. ROBERTS

JOVE BOOKS, NEW YORK

THE BERKLEY PUBLISHING GROUP
Published by the Penguin Group
Penguin Group (USA) LLC
375 Hudson Street, New York, New York 10014

USA • Canada • UK • Ireland • Australia • New Zealand • India • South Africa • China

penguin.com

A Penguin Random House Company

THE COUNTERFEIT GUNSMITH

A Jove Book / published by arrangement with the author

JOVE® is a registered trademark of Penguin Group (USA) LLC.
The "J" design is a trademark of Penguin Group (USA) LLC.

For information, address: The Berkley Publishing Group,
a division of Penguin Group (USA) LLC,
375 Hudson Street, New York, New York 10014.

ISBN: 978-0-515-15496-2

PUBLISHING HISTORY
Jove mass-market edition / September 2014

PRINTED IN THE UNITED STATES OF AMERICA

10 9 8 7 6 5 4 3 2 1

Cover illustration by Sergio Giovine.

ONE

Jeremy Pike looked at the hundred-dollar bill in his hand. He turned it over a few times, snapped it to test its strength, then put it down on the desk in front of him. The man he was seated across from picked it up and leaned back in his chair.

"Whataya think, Pike?" the other man asked.

"It looks damn good," Pike said, "but it's a fake."

"Are you sure?"

"I'm positive."

The older man regarded him intently for a moment, then said, "Well, you're right. It is fake. And it's all over the country."

Pike stared back at the Secretary of the Treasury.

"Why am I here, Mr. Secretary?"

"We need somebody to go out there and find out who's making these," the Secretary said.

"Why me?"

"Frankly?"

"Please, sir."

"West and Gordon are on other assignments and unavailable," the Secretary said.

"So I'm your third choice?"

"Basically, yes."

Pike thought about that, then shrugged and said, "I guess I can live with that."

"Good."

"Where did this particular bill come from?"

"It and a bunch like it were picked up in Missouri," the Secretary said. "Saint Louis, to be exact."

"Was an arrest made?"

"Unfortunately," the Secretary said, "the gentleman who was passing these fake bills was killed when the bills were confiscated."

"I see," Pike said. "Sir, am I supposed to work alone on this?"

"Unless you can draft someone into your service," the Secretary said. "Of course, at the time that you are ready to make an arrest, we can send in some military assistance for you."

"I appreciate that, sir," Pike said.

The Secretary opened the top drawer of his desk, took out a white envelope, and tossed it over to Pike's side of the desk.

"Traveling money," he said. "If you find you need more, let me know, and you'll be able to pick it up at any bank."

"Sir." Pike grabbed up the envelope and tucked it into his jacket pocket.

"That's all," the Secretary said. "Stay in touch."

"Directly, sir?"

"Mr. Jenks will liaise between us," the Secretary said. "Do you know Jenks?"

"I do, sir."

"You don't like him?"

"I do not, sir."

"Hardly matters, does it?"

"No, sir."

"He's waiting for you outside."

"Yes, sir."

Pike stood up and left the office. The Secretary had been in Federal service for over thirty years, and had always been a man of few words and much candor. Pike appreciated that.

Adam Jenks was, indeed, waiting for Pike outside the Secretary's office. Jenks was in his thirties, had been working in the Treasury Department for ten years. As far as Pike knew, nobody liked him. Maybe not even the Secretary.

"Pike."

"Jenks."

"I have your travel papers." Jenks handed him a brown envelope. "Also the file on what we know so far."

"Thanks."

"You will dispose of the file after you've read it, of course."

"Of course."

"Your train leaves first thing tomorrow morning."

"Doesn't give me much time to draft any help, does it?" Pike asked. "Unless you want to come along."

"Please," Jenks said. "I know my limitations, Pike. I'd probably get us both killed."

Pike actually found a little more respect for the man after he said that.

"I'll walk you out," Jenks said.

Outside they stopped just in front of the Treasury Building.

"Try not to mess this up, Pike," Jenks said.

"Thanks, Jenks."

"For what?"

"For reminding me why I don't like you."

"Please," Jenks said, and went back inside.

TWO

"Call."

Clint Adams tossed his chips into the pot without looking at his cards again. He knew very well what was in his hand. He set the five cards down on the table and waited to see what the other players would do.

The first to act had been Jack Denim. He had made his fifty-dollar bet with a confident smile.

Clint called.

There were three other players.

Barry Cord looked at the cards in his hand. They hadn't changed.

"I fold," he said.

Tom Curry had already set his cards down on the table, but now he lifted the corners to look again. The telltale sign of a man who had nothing.

"I'm out."

The dealer of that particular hand was a local gambler named Crane, Henry Crane. He had his five cards in his hand, closed rather than fanned out. Clint watched his body language, his eyes. He never looked at the cards again.

"I call," he said, "and raise fifty."

The original bettor, Denim, stared at Crane.

"What are you holdin'?" he asked.

"Pay and see," Crane said.

"Oh, I call," Denim said, peeking at his cards first. "And I raise a hundred."

Then he looked at Clint. "Your play, Adams."

Clint had not raised because he'd felt sure that Crane would. Now he felt sure he knew the strength of each man's hand.

"I'll call both raises," Clint said, "and add one of my own."

Denim glared at him.

"But you didn't raise when I did," he said. "All you did was call."

Clint looked at the man. He was a townsman, not a gambler. Crane was a professional gambler. He was the one Clint had to beware of.

"It's my play," Crane said. "Adams, you're makin' this interestin'."

"That's my aim, Crane."

"Well," Crane said, "let's keep it interestin', then. I call and raise."

"Sonofabitch!" Denim said.

"Your play, Mr. Denim," Crane said.

"You fellas are workin' together against me!" Denim said.

Crane's face went cold.

"That sounds like a real uncomfortable accusation that we're cheatin', friend. That ain't what you mean, is it?"

"Relax, Crane," Clint said. "Mr. Denim didn't mean that, did you, Denim?"

Denim actually looked like he was pouting.

"I just—I just meant—"

"Never mind," Crane said. "What are you going to do, Denim?"

The townsman frowned, looked pained, and then dropped his cards on the table, facedown. "I'm gonna fold."

"Adams?" Crane asked.

"Well," Clint said, "we could go round and round with this again, but I'll just call so we can move on."

"Okay, there you go," Crane said. He laid his cards out. "I got a pair of aces."

"What?" Denim said, shocked. "I had that beat!"

Clint laid his cards down.

"Two pairs, tens over threes."

Denim groaned, "I had that beat, too."

"Then you should've called," Crane said. "Good hand, Adams. Well played."

"Thanks, Crane."

It was a quiet afternoon in the Blue Owl Saloon, which was on the Saint Louis waterfront. Clint had found this to be more comfortable for him than some of the more expensive, high-class hotels in the city. Crane was his kind of poker player, Denim was annoying, but the other two men were dockworkers that he was comfortable with. And if any of them had recognized him, no one had made a comment.

As Denim picked up the cards and started to shuffle, the batwings swung in and a man wearing a badge entered.

"Who's that?" Crane asked.

Clint, who could see the door clearly, said, "Looks like the sheriff."

"This city's got a police department," Crane said.

"And a sheriff," Barry Cord informed them.

"What's the sheriff do?" Clint asked.

"Usually makes notifications of some kind," Tom Curry said.

"Well," Clint said, "he's coming over here for some reason."

"Deal the cards, Mr. Denim," Crane said.

Denim began to deal them out for another hand of five-card stud.

"Clint Adams?" the sheriff said when he reached the table.

"That's me," Clint said, scooping up his cards.

"Can we talk?" the tall, fortyish lawman asked.

Clint looked at his five totally mismatched cards, tossed them down, and said, "Might as well. I'm not going to be able to make anything out of these." He looked at the lawman. "Buy you a beer?"

THREE

When they were each standing at the bar with a beer in hand, the badge toter said, "My name is Sheriff Carl Kinkaid."

"Clint Adams," Clint said, "but you know that."

"I been lookin' for you in some of our town's better saloons," Kinkaid said.

"I find this place very comfortable," Clint said, "but what is it that got you searching for me?"

"The Saint Louis Police asked me to find you," the sheriff said. "They'd like you to come in and have a talk with them."

"About what?"

"That I don't know," Kinkaid said. "They just asked me to find you and . . . what did they say . . . oh yeah, invite you in for a talk."

"They didn't give you any indication of what it was about?" he asked.

"No," Kinkaid said, "but if it makes you feel better, I don't think they plan to arrest you."

"Well, that's good," Clint said, "because I haven't done anything to get arrested for."

"Glad to hear it."

"So I'll just finish this beer, collect my money, and you can show me where the police department is."

Kinkaid raised his mug and said, "Sounds like a plan."

Sheriff Kinkaid took Clint down to Market Street to Police Headquarters, and stopped at the bottom of the steps.

"Not coming in?" Clint asked.

"No," Kinkaid said. "I did my part. Thanks for the beer."

As the man walked away, Clint wondered, just for a moment, if he was walking himself into a bad situation on the word of a lawman he didn't know. But in the end he decided to just go on in and see what the story was.

He ascended the steps and approached the uniformed officer—a sergeant—who was manning the front desk.

"Help ya?" the man asked.

"My name is Clint Adams," Clint said. "Sheriff Kinkaid asked me to come here."

"Who do you want to see?"

"Well," Clint said, "I guess that depends on who wants to see me."

The sergeant frowned, then sighed.

"Stay here, I'll check."

Clint remained standing at the desk and the sergeant soon returned with a young man wearing a charcoal gray suit.

"Mr. Adams?"

"That's right."

"A pleasure, sir," the man said, extending his hand for Clint to shake. "I'm Detective Edward Donnelly."

"Detective."

"Thank you very much for coming."

"Curiosity got the better of me."

"Well, I'm sure we can take care of that," Donnelly said. "Why don't you follow me?"

As they started down a hallway, Clint asked, "Are we going to see your boss?"

"No," Donnelly said, "we're going to my desk."

"But I thought—"

"That somebody in authority wanted to see you?" Donnelly asked. "I'm sorry, it was just me."

"But the sheriff—"

"Yes," Donnelly said over his shoulder, "I visited the sheriff and asked him to find you for me."

"So . . . your boss doesn't know about this meeting?"

As they reached a desk, Donnelly turned and said, "Mmm, not yet. Have a seat."

The detective sat behind his desk. Clint took a chair alongside it. Around them other men sat at desks, some alone, some with people they were questioning.

"What's this about?"

"Many of these detectives are working on a case involving counterfeit hundred-dollar bills," Donnelly said. "Some of them are looking for the men who are passing them. Still others are looking for whoever's making them."

"But you have a different idea."

"Yes, I do."

"How does that involve me?"

"There's a man in town who says he knows you."

"Who?"

"He says his name is Joshua Jones."

"I don't know any Joshua Jones."

"Well, I don't think that's his real name," Donnelly said.

"Who do you think he is?"

"I don't know," Donnelly said. "Maybe somebody who can help me."

"So what do you want from me?"

"I want you to tell me who Joshua Jones really is."

"How would I know?"

"Well," Donnelly said, "he says he knows you. Maybe you know him. All you have to do is see him."

Clint thought about the request. It seemed simple enough.

"Okay," Clint said, "trot him on out here and I'll take a look at him."

"Well, he's not right here, in this building," Donnelly said, "but I can take you to him."

"Is he far from here?"

"Not far," Donnelly said. "He's in the hospital."

FOUR

Detective Donnelly got them a one-horse buggy and a uniformed police driver to take them to the hospital.

"Wait here," he told the man when they got out.

"Yes, sir."

Donnelly led Clint into the hospital, down a hallway to a set of stairs, and up to the second floor. Along the way, they walked past white-clad doctors and nurses, patients walking in the halls, and even some visitors.

"This room here," Donnelly said, pointing to a closed door. There was another uniformed officer seated in a chair alongside it. He nodded to Donnelly.

"Should I go in alone?"

"Why?"

"Well," Clint said, "if you think he's not giving you his real name, why would that change if you walk in there with me now?"

"Hmm, I see what you mean. All right, then, Mr. Adams,

go on in and see what you can find out," Donnelly said. "I'll be right here if you need me."

"Okay, Detective."

Clint turned to go in, but Donnelly called out to him again.

"Adams?"

"Yeah?"

"Maybe I should hold on to your gun."

"Detective," Clint said, "if that's a condition of me going in, then we might as well forget it now."

"Mr. Adams—"

"I don't give up my gun, Detective," Clint said. "Not under any circumstances."

"But—"

"If you know who I am," Clint went on, "then you'll understand why."

Donnelly stood there for a moment, thinking, then said, "Well, okay, then. Go on in."

Clint turned to the door and opened it. When he entered, the man in the bed, who was sitting up, staring out the window, turned to look at him.

"Clint."

"Hello, Jeremy."

Jeremy Pike had a bandage across his chest and down one arm. He had another on his head, but Clint was certainly able to recognize the man who was a member of the President's Secret Service.

"How'd you find out I was here?" Pike asked.

Clint approached the bed.

"The law," Clint said. "In fact, they're outside the door right now."

"Yeah, I know," he said.

"Well, you apparently mentioned me to someone. Detective Donnelly?"

"Yes, that's right."

"And he asked the sheriff to find me, which he did. I went to see Donnelly and he asked me to come and see you. So are you supposed to be Joshua Jones?"

"Ah, yes . . ."

"Why the phony name?"

"I'm working," Pike said.

"Under the name 'Joshua Jones,'" Clint said. "So that's not just a name you gave the police."

"No," he said. "That's my cover name."

"So okay," Clint said. "You came to Saint Louis as Joshua Jones to work on an assignment."

"Right."

"Obviously, something went wrong."

"Right again."

"And you ended up here," Clint said. "What happened?"

"I got jumped, and beat up, and kind of . . . shot."

"Kind of?"

"Well, okay, shot."

"In the chest?"

"Yeah," Pike said, "high up on the left side. They left me for dead."

"But you didn't die."

"No, somebody got me here in time."

"Who?"

"I'm not sure."

"When did this happen?"

"A few days ago."

"Why not tell the police what's going on?"

"I don't know who I can trust in the police department," Pike said.

"Donnelly seems like a decent young man."

"Yeah, well, he doesn't have much authority," Pike said. "In fact, I'm surprised he got you here. He was ordered not to bother."

"Is that right?" Clint asked. "Seems not very good at taking orders, then."

"Well," Pike said, "he's got that in his favor anyway."

"So tell me," Clint said, "how did you even know I was in Saint Louis?"

"That's kind of a story."

Clint sat on the edge of the bed and said, "It's my guess that's why I'm here."

FIVE

Jeremy Pike had arrived in Saint Louis by train, traveling under the name "Joshua Jones." He'd registered at a hotel down near the docks, and started doing his drinking in the Blue Owl Saloon. The reason was that the file Jenks had given him said that the dead counterfeiter—or the man who was working for the counterfeiter—did his drinking there.

"For a few days all I did was drink, and listen," Pike said. "Eventually, I wasn't considered a stranger in the place, and patrons went back to talking. I managed to identify two men I thought would get me what I wanted."

"The counterfeiters."

"Yeah," Pike said, "these two weren't smart enough to make the bills, but they were dumb enough to do the grunt work and talk about it. And flash the money they were being paid."

"The money they were paid with?" Clint asked.

"You guessed it," Pike said. "Counterfeit. They weren't even smart enough to know that."

"You got hold of one of the bills?"

Pike nodded.

"When the bartender wasn't looking," Pike said. "So I started tailing them."

"And?"

"They led me to another man."

"One of the counterfeiters?"

"The paymaster," Pike said. "His name is Tom Colby. He's the one who pays the other two to do their work."

"Which is?"

"To pass the bills," Pike said, "get them into circulation."

"And what's Colby doing when he's not the paymaster?" Clint asked.

"He has a store," Pike said. "Sells farming equipment. He also sits on the city council."

"That's handy."

"Once I pinpointed him, I started watching him and forgot about the other two. That was my mistake."

"They're the ones who shot you?"

Pike nodded.

"They're pretty dumb, but apparently they know how to do their job."

"Apparently not," Clint said.

"How so?"

"Well," Clint said, "you're still alive."

"True," Pike said.

"So how did the police get onto you?"

"I'm not sure," Pike said. "When I woke up, I was here, the police were here, and they were asking me who I am."

"And they know about the counterfeiting."

"Obviously," Pike said.

"So what do you want me to do?" Clint asked. "Intervene on your behalf? I don't have any leverage here."

"No, not that," Pike said. "I want you to pick up where I left off."

"You want me to do your job?"

Pike winced.

"Well, when you put it that way, it sounds bad," he said, "but yeah."

"You don't have a partner for this assignment?" Clint asked. "West? Gordon? O'Grady?"

"They're on other assignments," Pike said. "I was sent in alone, but I was approved to recruit any help that I need. So I'm recruiting you."

"Are you going to wave the flag at me, Pike?"

"Hell, Clint," Pike said, "I'll wrap you up in it if I have to."

Clint didn't reply.

"Look," Pike said, "I'm going to be laid up for a while. I could call in and get somebody to replace me, but they'd have to start from scratch. You're already here, and in place at the Blue Owl. Also, I don't relish calling my boss and telling him I messed this up."

"You never told me how you knew I was here."

"Simple," Pike said, "I saw you at the Blue Owl."

"When?"

"Last week."

"I never saw you."

"That's because I'm normally good at my job," the Secret Service man said. "I just happened to slip up once."

"And almost got killed for it."

Pike put his right hand to his head and then his shoulder, and said, "Too damn close."

"So you want me to go in and finish this up alone," Clint said.

"I'll give you the same approval they gave me—recruit

anybody you want to help you, just make sure it's some-body you can trust."

"I can think of a couple of people," Clint said, "but it would take them a while to get here."

"Nobody local?"

"I haven't been here long enough to meet somebody I'd trust that much," Clint said.

"Clint," Pike said, "I need your help on this."

"How long are you going to be laid up exactly?" Clint asked. "Do you know?"

"Not exactly," Pike said, "but I might be able to get out in time to help you."

There was a knock on the door and Detective Donnelly called out, "Everything okay in there?"

"Fine," Clint called. "I'll be right out." He looked at Pike. "What do I tell him?"

"Do you trust him?"

"I just met him," Clint said, "so no."

"Then we can't tell him who I really am."

"Who do we tell him you are," Clint said, "and how do we tell him you know me? And what you wanted with me?"

"I've been lying here thinking about that," Pike said, "just in case they did get you here."

"And?"

"Well," Pike said, "I haven't exactly come up with a good cover story for us. Yet."

"Yet?"

"I'm still working on it."

"In that case," Clint said, looking over at the door, "I suggest you come up with something pretty quick."

SIX

When Clint came walking out of the room, both Detective Donnelly and the uniformed policeman looked at him expectantly.

"Well?" Donnelly asked.

"Well," Clint said, "he knew who I was."

"Yes," Donnelly said, "but do you know him?"

Clint hesitated.

"Well?"

"Yes . . . and no."

"What's that mean?"

Clint looked around.

"Why don't we get out of the hall and talk about it?" he asked.

Donnelly looked around, then said, "There's a saloon around the corner that the doctors and nurses use."

"That sounds good."

Donnelly looked at the policeman.

"Keep your eye on that door!"

"Yes, sir."

"Come on," Donnelly said to Clint.

Around the corner they got two beers at the bar and then grabbed a table. The customers in the small saloon were mostly doctors and nurses.

"Okay," Donnelly said, "so tell me about Joshua Jones."

"I met Jones a few years ago," Clint said.

Donnelly waited, and when nothing else was forthcoming, he said. "And?"

"That's it," Clint said. "We met. I'm not even exactly sure how. Might have been at a poker table."

"Then why did he ask for you?" Donnelly asked. "How did he know you were in town?"

"He said he saw me on the street a few days ago," Clint said.

"And what does he want from you?"

"Well, for some reason he thinks I have some influence with the law," Clint said. "He wants me to get you to let him go."

"He's not going anywhere for a while," Donnelly said. "At least, not until he heals."

"I'm sure he meant after that."

"Did he say anything to you about counterfeiting?" the detective asked.

"No, and I didn't mention it," Clint said. "Wasn't sure you wanted me to."

"Quite right," Donnelly said. He sat back, played with his beer mug. "So this is a bust."

"I guess so," Clint said. "I don't know what else I can tell you."

"Did Jones say where he saw you? On what street?"

"Somewhere down by the docks."

"What's a man like you doing down by the docks?"

"Where should a man like me be?"

"Someplace a little higher class."

"I don't know what you've heard about me, Detective," Clint said, "but I'm very comfortable drinking down on the docks."

"Drinking where?"

"The Blue Owl."

"That's kind of a rough place," Donnelly said. "What else are you doing there?"

"Playing poker."

"And where are you staying?" Donnelly asked.

"The Mayflower."

"Oh," Donnelly said.

"What?"

"That's more like it."

"I said I liked drinking and playing poker down near the docks," Clint said. "I didn't say I wanted to sleep there."

SEVEN

Clint and Donnelly left the saloon together.

"I told Jones I'd bring him some things," Clint said. "A razor, some food . . . is that okay?"

"Yes," Donnelly said. "I'll tell the men at the door to allow you inside."

"Thanks."

"Why would you do that for him?"

"Why not?" Clint asked. "Who else has he got in town?"

Donnelly shrugged.

"If I need you, I know where to find you."

"I'll help you in any way I can, Detective."

"Thank you."

"By the way," Clint said as the detective started to leave.

"Yes?"

"How did you find out about the counterfeiting? And do you know who's doing it?"

"That's not something I can discuss with you, Mr. Adams," the young detective said.

"I see."

"Good day."

Donnelly walked to the buggy and told the driver to take him back to Police Headquarters.

Clint went to his hotel, got cleaned up, then went out and bought a razor and some food for "Joshua Jones." That much was true. But Pike wanted him to come back so they could talk more about the assignment, without the detective right outside the door.

"At that time," Pike had said, "you can tell me your final decision."

It was a few hours before he returned. By then there was a different policeman at the door.

"Clint Adams," he said to the man. He raised the bag he was holding. "I brought some things for the patient."

"Okay," the policeman said, "you can go in."

Clint entered the room. Once again Pike looked away from the window at him.

"Is that what I think it is?" he asked.

"A steak sandwich."

"Oh, that's great!" Pike exclaimed.

Clint crossed to the bed and handed the bag to Pike.

"Be careful sticking your hand in there," he said. "There's also a straight-edged razor."

While Pike hauled out the steak sandwich and tucked into it, Clint pulled a chair over.

"Did the detective tell you anything?" Pike asked.

"No," Clint said. "He said he wasn't able to discuss the counterfeiting case with me."

Pike nodded and chewed.

"Did the Treasury Department know that the Saint Louis Police were working on the case?"

"No," Pike said, "I had no idea when I got here. In fact, I had no idea until I woke up here and the police started interrogating me."

"How wide has the distribution of the bills gone?" Clint asked.

"Not sure," Pike said. "We know it started here. It's probably moved on to all the adjoining states."

"Anyone working there?"

"No," Pike said, "it really is just me working on this."

Clint nodded.

"Unless you've decided to come aboard?"

"What if you sent a telegram to Washington and asked for another man?"

"That'd be admitting I couldn't handle it myself," Pike said. "I've been building a reputation for too long to ruin it now. I'd never get another assignment. I'll be assisting others—West, O'Grady—for the rest of my life."

"I understand."

"This is pretty good," Pike said of the sandwich. "Where'd you get it?"

"Down the street from my hotel."

"Which is?"

"The Mayflower."

Pike's eyebrows went up. "I'm staying in a flophouse down by the docks," he said. "Part of my cover."

"I hope you don't expect me to do that."

"No," Pike said, "it's already established who you are, and where you're staying. I don't think the counterfeiting ring members would ever expect that you're looking for them."

"And for that reason," Clint said, "you think I have a good chance of finding them."

"Exactly." Pike swallowed what he was chewing, stared longingly at the last bite in his hand. "That is, if you agree to work with me."

Clint studied Pike while the man ate the last bite, then sighed and said, "All right, tell me everything you know—and don't leave anything out."

EIGHT

Pike told Clint the names of the two men who had left him for dead. Clint was surprised that he knew one of them.

"You know him?" Pike asked.

"Oh, yeah."

"Well, that's good," Pike said. "But . . . you don't want to give yourself away too soon."

"Don't worry," Clint said, "I won't. Now, where do I find this paymaster?"

"Tom Colby has a store on Washington Street," Pike said. "I don't know how you can get in there—"

"I'll figure something out."

"I can tell you he drinks at a place called the Royale Saloon."

"Okay," Clint said. "I can use that."

"Do you need to see one of the bills?" Pike asked.

"That would probably help me in identifying them when I see them," Clint said. "You don't have one here, do you?"

"No," Pike said, "you'll have to go to my hotel to see

them. I've got a few bills hidden there. I'll tell you
where . . ."

Clint left the hospital shaking his head. He'd first met Jeremy Pike through his friend Jim West a few years before.
Since then he'd run into the man once or twice, worked
with him one other time. He liked him, considered him a
friend, but not one of his good friends. That title was saved
for men like West and Wyatt Earp and Bat Masterson.

But Pike had asked him for his help, and Clint didn't
feel he could turn the man down. Especially since Pike
was in no condition to finish the assignment himself. And
it was, after all, for the government.

So his time in Saint Louis to play poker and just relax
was over.

He caught a cab and had it take him right to Pike's hotel,
down by the docks. He was able to bypass the front desk
because Pike had given him the room key.

The hotel was the perfect example of a flophouse. It
was on the verge of falling down, perhaps held up only by
the horrible smell.

He made his way to the second floor and found room
nine. Looking both ways in the hall, he used the key and
let himself in.

He didn't know if Pike was a slob, or if the condition
of the room was also part of his cover. Knowing the man,
he figured it was the latter, because Pike—under normal
circumstances—was a pretty spiffy dresser.

He closed the door behind him and looked around. Pike
told him he had hidden some bills behind a drawer in the
beat-up dresser by the window. He went to the dresser,
pulled out the first and second drawers. When he pulled

the bottom drawer all the way out, he found an envelope behind it. He left the drawer on the floor and took three bills out of the envelope. He examined all three, holding them up to the sunlight. They were very, very good. In the end he put two back, reinserted the drawer, and stuck the third into his pocket. He thought he might be able to press it into service as his bona fides if the need arose.

For a moment he considered sitting down, but he didn't want to risk catching anything. He was about to leave when there was a knock at the door.

He hesitated, then decided to do what came naturally when someone knocked on a door.

He opened it.

NINE

"Are you Jones?"

The person asking him the question was a girl—a young woman, actually. She appeared to be in her twenties, was tall with long black hair, and was wearing a jacket and trousers that had seen better days but were, at least, clean. She was better than the hotel they were standing in.

"Well?" she asked.

She was also wearing a gun on her hip, worn like she knew how to use it.

"If I am," he said, "are you going to shoot me?"

"Why would I shoot you?"

"I don't know," he said. "I'm just not used to seeing a girl wear a gun."

"I've got to protect myself."

"This is Saint Louis," he said, "not the Wild West."

"Believe me," she said, "there's a lot in this town I need protection from. But no, I'm not gonna shoot you."

"Then I'm Jones."

"I may not shoot you," she said, "but I might kick you in the ass!"

Clint wondered if this was someone Pike should have told him about. Then again, she wouldn't be asking him if he was "Jones" if she knew Pike.

"Who are you?"

"Who am I?" she asked. "I'm your contact."

"Do you have a name?" he asked. "Or is that your name? Contact?"

"'Course I got a name, ya damned fool!" she said. "It's Isabel."

"Isabel?"

"What's wrong with it?"

"Nothing," Clint said, "it just doesn't, uh, seem to suit you."

"Well," she said, "most of my friends just call me Izzy."

"Izzy," Clint said. "Yeah, that fits better. Do you want to come in, Izzy?"

"God, no," she said, peering past him. "This place is a dump."

"Yeah, it is," he said. "I'm going to move soon."

"Let's go somewhere else and talk," she suggested.

"Okay," he said, "but you pick it."

"I know a place," she said. "It's near here. Come on, you can follow me."

He stepped out into the hall, closed the door, and locked it.

She laughed.

"What?"

"That ain't gonna stop anybody who wants to get in."

"Doesn't matter, really," he said. "There's nothing in there to steal."

She nodded, then led the way along the hall and down-stairs to the lobby.

Izzy took Clint to a nearby saloon, not a particularly high-class establishment but several steps up from the Blue Owl down on the docks.

They went right to the bar and the girl ordered two beers.

"Izzy," the beefy bartender said, "I thought I tol' you not to come in here, girl."

"Hey, Bronco," she said, "it ain't like I'm unaccompanied, is it? My friend, here, would like a beer."

Bronco looked at Clint, who just stared back at the man. Eventually the bartender got the message and drew two mugs of beer for them.

"Come on," Izzy said, grabbing both beers and leading the way to a table in the back. The small saloon was about half full, and all the men looked after Izzy as she went by.

She set the beers down on either side of the table and sat down. Clint sat across from her, put his left hand around the mug.

"Want to tell me what we're doing here?" he asked.

"You was waitin' for a contact, right?" she asked. "Well, I'm it."

Clint stared at the girl, wondering what was going on. Was this on the level, or was she trying to horn in on something, like drinking in the saloon when the bartender warned her to stay away?

"What is it I need a contact for?" he asked.

"Why don't you tell me?" she demanded.

Clint sat back and sipped his beer, continuing to regard the girl, who started to squirm.

"You don't know a thing, do you?" he asked.

"Whataya mean?"

"You're bluffing," he said. "You're trying to get something out of me for nothing."

"Hey," she said, "I don't gotta put up with—I'm just tryin' ta help."

"Yeah, but help who?" he asked.

"Look, how would I know your name is Jones?"

"I registered at my hotel as Jones."

"Then how would I know you need a contact?"

"Like I said," Clint said, "you're bluffing. Maybe you heard me saying something in another saloon. Who the hell are you?"

Suddenly she stiffened, and he thought she was a split second from drawing her gun.

"Don't think about it," he said. "I'd kill you before you drew."

She pulled her right hand away from her gun like it burned.

"Put that hand on your beer."

She wrapped her right hand around the mug.

"Now tell me what this is about."

"I'm—I'm—" She paused to sip the beer, wetting her lips. "I'm just tryin' ta make some money. You got somethin' goin', and I thought I could get in on it."

"What do you bring to the table?"

"Huh?"

"Why would I need you?"

"I know my way around," she said.

"The docks?"

"The docks, the county, the city," she said. "I know Saint Louis—and I know the underbelly."

He smiled, almost laughed.

"What do you know about the underbelly of anything?" he asked.

She frowned, almost pouted.

"I know how things work."

"Why don't I ask that bartender if you know how things work?" he asked.

"Don't!" she snapped.

"Why? What would he tell me?"

She tightened her lips.

"What's he to you?"

Grudgingly, she said, "He's my uncle."

"Ah . . ."

She looked over at the bar, where the bartender was glowering over at them.

"Doesn't look like he likes me," Clint said.

"Look, Mr. Jones—"

"Thanks for the beer, Izzy," he said, standing up.

"Wait!"

"Izzy," he said, "you shouldn't walk around wearing that gun."

"I can use it," she insisted. "If you need help, just let me know. You can ask for me here."

Clint nodded, headed for the door, but detoured to the bar first.

"She really your niece?" he asked Bronco.

"She is."

"She's looking for trouble."

"You're tellin' me."

"She knows how to use that gun?"

"Oh, she can shoot," Bronco said. "She's just got no sense."

"Then maybe you ought to give her some."

"Believe me, I've tried," Bronco said. "What's your interest?"

"None," Clint said. "She said she had something for me, but she doesn't."

"She's pretty young, you know."

"I told you," Clint said, "I'm not interested."

Bronco stood up straight and said, "Why not? What's wrong with her?"

"Is there a woman in her life?" Clint asked. "Mother? Aunt?"

"No," Bronco said, "no woman."

"There should be," Clint said. "Somebody needs to get through to her before she *finds* trouble."

The bartender seemed to deflate.

"I'll try."

"I need to pay for those beers."

"No," the bartender said. "On the house."

Clint nodded, and walked to the batwing doors.

TEN

Clint left the small saloon and went back to his own hotel. Normally, he would have been at the Blue Owl, playing poker. Perhaps not doing that was not a good idea. He needed to maintain a low profile, especially now that he was working for the government—sort of.

He wanted to talk to Pike again about the hundred-dollar bill in his pocket, but he decided to do that in the morning. So after just a short time in his room, he left and headed for the Blue Owl.

The game was ongoing as he entered, the gambler Henry Crane still in place. The other seats had been taken over by different men. Clint approached and sat down in the empty chair.

"Thought I was saving that chair in vain," Crane said. "Welcome back."

"What, no Denim?" Clint asked as the men finished their hand. "You manage to bust Jack out?"

"I think he just went to get some more money," Crane said, raking in his pot. "You got here just in time to deal."

Clint gathered up the cards and shuffled. He'd been hoping to find Denim there. But if he was any judge of men—and he thought he was—the man would be back to play.

"Coming out," he said. "Five-card stud."

As he'd expected, Jack Denim showed up about two hours later. By then, two of the other chairs had emptied, so Denim took one of them.

"Got some more money?" Crane asked him.

"I got plenty of money, don't you worry," Denim said. He pulled a sheaf of bills from his pocket, some of them hundreds.

Hundreds.

Clint looked at them lying on the table, and couldn't tell if they were real or not. But Denim was one of the names Pike had given him. Denim and another man had beaten and shot him, and left Pike for dead. Now here he was with a bunch of hundred-dollar bills.

Clint was just going to have to win some of those bills from him, and then take them to Pike. The Secret Service man would know if they were real or not.

"Okay," Crane said, "ante up, boys."

ELEVEN

"Buy you a beer?" Crane asked.

The game was over for the night. They hadn't cleaned Denim out, but Clint had managed to get a few of his hundred-dollar bills.

"Sure, why not?"

They went to the bar. The place had pretty much emptied out, except for a couple of drunks at tables finishing up their last drinks.

"Two beers," Crane said to the bartender.

"Closin' up," the man said, giving them their beers. "Soon as those two are done."

"Fine," Crane said.

"So how much longer do you intend to stay in Saint Louis?" Clint asked.

Crane shrugged, said, "Oh, I don't know. I'm doing okay here."

"You're picking up pennies here at the Blue Owl," Clint said. "There are other saloons with bigger games."

Crane sipped his beer.

"What is it?" Clint asked. "Are you hiding out?"

"Actually," Crane said, "yeah."

"From the law?"

"Oh, no," Crane said, "nothing like that."

Clint waited, but when Crane didn't say anything else, he said, "Look, you don't have to explain anything to me."

"No, it's okay," Crane said. "I didn't expect to run into anyone like you here."

"Like me?"

"I mean, somebody who knows the game," Crane said. "Actually knows how it's played."

"You're a good poker player," Clint said. "You must have played against good players before."

"Yeah, I did," Crane said. "In fact, I was in a big game a couple of months ago. In Denver."

"With who?"

"Among others, Bat Masterson, Luke Short, coupla fellas named Brady and Brett. A few others."

"And what happened?"

Crane looked chagrined.

"They cleaned me out," he said. "Taught me a lesson, I'm afraid."

"So you just build yourself another stake and try again," Clint said.

"That's what I'm tryin' to do."

"Here?"

Crane smiled.

"I'm startin' small," he said.

"You sure are," Clint said. "Seems to me your skills are sharp."

"Maybe . . ."

"You have doubts?"

"I did," Crane said, "after that game. They sent me away with my tail between my legs, and two bits for a beer. That was hard to take."

"Consider the men you were playing against," Clint said. "I've lost to them myself . . . plenty of times."

"Time to go, gents," the bartender said.

The two drunks had finished their drinks and were shuffling toward the door.

"Okay," Crane said. He and Clint tossed off the remainder of their beers.

Outside Crane asked, "How much longer will you be in Saint Louis?"

"A few days, at least."

"And you'll play?"

"When I can."

"Good," Crane said. "At least I'll have you to hone my skills against."

"Which way are you going?" Clint asked.

"My rooming house is that way," Crane said, pointing.

"So's my hotel."

They started walking together.

"How much do you know about Jack Denim?" Clint asked. Both Crane and Denim were already in the game when Clint first arrived.

"Not much," Crane said. "He lives in town, plays poker badly, but always seems to have the money to play. Unlike me, he gets cleaned out and keeps coming back."

"Maybe he's just too dumb to realize how outclassed he is," Clint said.

"Meaning I was outclassed?"

"At that time you were," Clint said. "When you play again, you won't be."

"That would be nice."

They approached Clint's hotel.

"What's your interest in Denim?" Crane asked.

"Just wondering where he gets the money to keep coming back."

"He must have a good job."

"Do you know what that would be?"

"No idea."

"This is my hotel," Clint said.

"Then I'll see you tomorrow," Crane said. "Get a good night's sleep. I'll want you at your best."

"I'm always at my best," Clint promised.

TWELVE

Clint removed his boots when he got to his room, hung his gun belt on the bedpost. He sat on the bed, took out the hundred-dollar bills he'd won off Denim, and the one he'd taken from Pike's room.

Briefly he had considered spending the night in Pike's hotel room, but the memory of how it looked and smelled changed his mind.

He lined the bills up on the bed in front of him and examined them. He took out a real hundred and laid it alongside. He was no expert, and it was hard to see the difference. He put the real one away in his pocket, then set the phony ones aside, not wanting to mix them in with his own money.

He was preparing to turn in for the night when there was a knock at his door. He doubted that the girl, Izzy, could have followed him there without him noticing her. Slipping his gun from his holster, he kept it in his right hand as he approached his door.

"Who is it?"

There was no immediate answer, and then a timid female voice said, "Uh, Mr. Adams?"

"That's right."

"Um, my name is Aurora Lane. I'd like to speak with you."

Clint cracked the door and peered out. A very pretty redhead with green eyes stared back at him.

"I don't know you," he said.

"No, sir," she said, "but if you let me in, we can fix that."

"Did someone send you?"

She frowned.

"You're very suspicious."

"Well, it's late," he said, "and a beautiful woman I've never seen before is knocking on my door."

"Is that an unusual occurrence for you?"

"At this time of night," he answered, "I would have to say yes."

"I can assure you," she said, "I mean you no harm."

Clint studied her for a moment, then opened the door all the way and peered out, looking both ways.

"May I come in?"

"If you're not worried about your reputation."

"Pooh," she said. "Reputations are a bother. I'm sure a man such as yourself realizes that."

"All right," he said, backing away, "come in."

She entered with a swish of fabric and he closed the door, turned to face her. She was wearing a green dress that made her eyes pop, held a shawl over shoulders that were bare.

"You look familiar," he said.

"Have you been to the Lulu Belle?" she asked.

"Once," he said, "when I first got to town." The Lulu Belle was a very high-class saloon and gambling house.

"You might have seen me there."

She looked like a woman who worked in a saloon, with her off-the-shoulder gown, lustrous long red hair, and carefully made-up face.

"Maybe that explains it," he said. "What brings you here?"

"I heard several of our customers talking about you being in town," she said.

"Is that a fact?" he asked. "And here I thought I was keeping a low profile."

"I suppose that's hard for a man with a reputation like yours," she said.

He walked to the bedpost and holstered his gun, feeling no danger from Aurora Lane.

"So you heard some men talking about me," he said. "How did you find me? And why?"

"How wasn't hard," she said. "Why is to warn you."

"About what?"

"That some men are plotting against you."

"Plotting?"

"Planning to kill you."

"How do you know that?"

"I heard them talking," she said. "Men tend to talk around saloon girls when they've had a few drinks. We become . . . invisible."

"I can't imagine you becoming invisible to any man," he told her.

She actually blushed and said, "Well, I . . . thank you very much."

"I guess I should thank you," he said. "Do you know the names of these men, or how they plan to do it?"

"I'm afraid I don't," she said. "I think one called another

Cal at one point, but that's all I know. I didn't hear them say how they were going to do it."

"How many of them are there?"

"Three," she said.

"And since you don't know their names, I suppose they're not regular customers?"

"No," she said, "they're not. In fact, I think they're strangers in town."

"Then who, I wonder, told them I was here?"

"I'm afraid I don't know that either," she said. She pulled the shawl more closely around her. "I'm afraid all I know is enough to warn you that someone wants to kill you."

"Are you cold?" he asked.

"No," she said, "excited."

"Excited?"

"Yes," she said. "If I took off this shawl, you'd see what I mean."

"It's exciting to come and warn someone that someone else wants to kill them?"

"No," she said, "it's exciting to be in the same room with the Gunsmith."

"Oh," he said, "well—"

"No, I didn't mean that," she said. "I mean, if you were the Gunsmith and you looked like an ogre . . . but you don't. You look . . . handsome."

"Well, thank you."

"You have a reputation . . . I mean, other than with a gun . . . with women. It makes a woman . . . curious."

"And excited."

She laughed and said, "Yes."

He tried to see through the shawl, to see what she was talking about.

"Stop that."

"Stop what?" he asked.

"Stop trying to see through my shawl."

"I'm sorry," he said, "it's just that you said—"

"Do you want to see?"

"Well . . . yes."

"All right."

With a shrug, she dropped the shawl to the floor. Immediately, he saw what she meant. She had large, round breasts and large nipples that were almost poking through the fabric of her dress.

"See?" she asked.

He wet his dry lips before saying, "Yes, I see."

Her skin was very pale, with a light dusting of freckles showing just a bit through her makeup. There were also some freckles on the swollen slopes of her breasts.

"Convinced?"

"Um, well, yeah."

"Now," she said, "maybe you'll satisfy the lady's curiosity."

"About . . ."

She took a few steps, bringing herself right up to him. He could feel the heat coming off her body.

"About you." She looked down at the obvious bulge in his pants. "Maybe you're a little excited at the moment, too?"

"Maybe," he said, his mouth still dry. He stared down at her cleavage. "Just a little."

THIRTEEN .

She placed her hand on his chest and stared up into his eyes. He put his hand on her rounded shoulders, felt her smooth skin with his palms. She slid her hand down over his belly, tugged on his belt, then felt the bulge through his pants.

"My, my," she said.

He ran his hands over the front of her gown, felt the hard nipples with his thumbs.

"Same here," he said.

"Are you going to kiss me?" she demanded.

He slid his arms around her, pulled her close, and kissed her. Her mouth opened and her tongue slid into his mouth. They kissed that way for a long time, their mouths fused together. When they broke apart, they were both breathless.

"Aurora . . ." he said.

"Clint . . ."

They kissed again, and this time they fell onto the bed,

limbs entwined. While they kissed, they pulled and tugged at each other's clothes until they were in a pile on the floor and their naked flesh was pressing together.

They rolled around on the bed for a while, getting to know each other's bodies by feel and taste. Her breasts were incredibly firm and smooth, but the amazing thing were those nipples. They were brown, large, with very wide areolas. He spent some time on them, enjoying the way they felt in his mouth.

She found enjoyment with his body, as well. Specifically his penis. It was hard and long, and she had to pry her nipple from his mouth so she could slither down between his legs and make love to his hard cock.

He rolled over onto his back to make it easier for her. She rubbed the smooth column of flesh against her even smoother cheeks, ran her nose along the length of him, inhaling his scent. Finally, she ran her tongue over it, wetting it thoroughly, before taking it into her hot mouth.

He moaned, reached down to cup her head with his hands as she bobbed up and down on him, sucking him. She slid her hands beneath him, cupping his balls, caressing them. As he lifted his hips, she took his buttocks into her hands as she continued to suck him.

When he felt he wouldn't be able to stand it anymore, he reached down for her. She resisted, but finally allowed him to slide from her wet mouth.

He pulled her up so she was lying on top of him, and kissed her again. Her breasts pressed against his chest, and he could feel her hard nipples. Trapped between them was his hard cock, and she began to run her pubic hair over him, up and down, until he could feel how wet she had become.

Abruptly, she sat up on him, stared at him, and lifted

her hips. She reached between them and guided his hard penis up into her. She was as hot as steam, and so slick he slid into her easily.

She gasped as he speared her, and she sat up straight, her hands pressed down on his sternum. She began to ride him that way, up and down, slowly at first, and grinding each time she came down, with a circular motion of her hips.

He reached out to hold her by the hips, but he couldn't keep his hands still. Her skin was so smooth and soft, he ran his hands all over her, coming back to her breasts. He cupped them, enjoying how heavy they were, and used his thumbs on her nipples. She gasped as she began to ride him faster and faster. He moved his hips with her, catching her rhythm, lifting himself to meet her each time she came down on him.

Her head dropped back so that he could see her long neck, and her breathing became ragged. She moved faster and faster, and he tried to stay with her as long as he could before he finally let out a roar and erupted inside her . . .

"Funny," she said moments later.

They were lying side by side on the bed, still naked.

"What's funny?" he asked.

"It seems like moments ago that we were strangers."

"It was moments ago."

"Well," she said, "maybe minutes . . . and yet here we are, naked together."

"Yes," Clint said, "here we are."

She lifted her head and looked at him.

"Are you sorry?"

"Not at all."

"Do you want me to leave?"

"Not at all."

"Good." She let her head fall back onto the pillow. "I'm very comfortable."

"Stay the night," he said.

"I can do that," she replied, "but if I do . . ."

"Yes?"

She reached out and let her hand fall onto his penis.

"I don't think we'll get much sleep."

"I wasn't thinking about sleeping."

FOURTEEN

In the morning Clint watched as Aurora dressed, covering up that glorious, pneumatic body with her gown and shawl.

"Come by the saloon later today," she said, leaning over him.

"I will," he promised.

She kissed him and slipped out.

He was tired from the night with her—she woke him three different times for more sex—but he forced himself to get up, wash, and dress. He put the phony hundreds—or the bills that Pike would identify as phony or not—into a pocket away from his own money, and left the room.

His hotel had a dining room that served a palatable breakfast. If he'd wanted a better meal, he would have gone to any one of a few cafés and restaurants he'd found in Saint Louis, but for now bacon and eggs in the hotel would suffice.

He ate slowly in the half-filled dining room, washing the food down with a full pot of coffee. Around him other diners—some hotel guests, others citizens of Saint

Louis—ate their breakfasts, paying him only the slightest attention. He'd been in Saint Louis long enough for the people to get used to the idea. That is, the people around his hotel, and in the Blue Owl.

He thought about what Aurora had told him the night before. There were three men in the city plotting to kill him. First, that sort of news was never a surprise to him. Second, he would be surprised if there weren't more than three. Aurora just happened to have heard these three discussing it.

Under normal circumstances, Clint watched his back diligently. After this, he'd have to watch it even more so. Also, since he was helping Pike. Suddenly, in the course of one day, everything about his stay in Saint Louis had changed.

Everything.

He left this hotel and caught a cab out front, telling the driver to take him to the hospital. When he arrived, he didn't go inside right away. He found a nearby café and bought some breakfast for Pike—the kind of breakfast they would not serve him in the hospital.

With the food in a bag, he returned to the hospital and made his way to Pike's room.

FIFTEEN

There was still a policeman seated by the door, and when Clint approached, he stood up.

"Clint Adams," Clint said.

"What's in the bag, sir?"

"Food."

"May I see?"

Clint allowed the man to look in the bag. The policeman frowned.

"What is that?"

"It's breakfast."

"Yes, but what—"

"There are three of them in there," Clint said. "Take one."

"Really?"

"I think two will be plenty for Mr. Jones," Clint said. "Go ahead."

"Thank you, sir."

The man took one out and unwrapped it.

"It's a biscuit," he said.

"I had them put some bacon and egg between it," Clint said

"I've never seen anything like this before. I mean, I've seen sandwiches—"

"Just enjoy it," Clint said, and went into the room.

"I thought I smelled something other than hospital food," Pike said.

"Here you go."

"I saved some coffee," Pike said, indicating a cup near his bed, on a table. "Don't know how warm it still is." He took the bag from Clint and looked inside.

"What is it?"

"Breakfast."

"Yes, but—" Pike took one out and unwrapped it. "A biscuit, but—"

"It's got egg and bacon in it," Clint said.

Pike took a bite.

"Wow," he said, "this could be very big. They did this?"

"It was my idea."

"You could get rich with an idea like this." Pike took another bite.

"Speaking of rich," Clint said, taking out the hundred-dollar bills he'd won from Denim.

"Are those the bills from my room?"

"No," Clint said, "I took these off Jack Denim in a poker game."

"Denim!" Pike said with distaste. "Let me see them."

Clint handed them over. Pike put his breakfast down and accepted the bills. He held them up to the light coming in through the window.

"Are they . . ." Clint said.

"Counterfeit."

"Show me."

"Look at this green line here, just at the top. See it?" Pike asked.

Clint squinted, then said, "Yeah, yeah, I see it. So that's it, huh?"

"That's it," Pike said. "If the counterfeiters discover it and fix it, we might never be able to tell the real bills from the fakes."

Clint took out the one bill he'd removed from Pike's room and looked at it. He saw the same green line.

"What's that?" Pike asked. He'd once again picked up his breakfast sandwich.

"This is one of the bills I took from your room," Clint said. "I left the others in place."

"That room was pretty bad, huh?"

"Awful," Clint said. "I don't know how you managed to sleep in there."

"Hey," Pike said, "undercover is undercover. But believe me, it wasn't easy."

"These bills are amazing," Pike said, fishing the second sandwich out of the bag. "I can't wait to catch this guy to find out how he does it. Do you want this one?"

"No," Clint said, "I bought three, one for the policeman outside and two for you."

"Ah," Pike said, "making friends."

"It never hurts," Clint said.

"What about Denim?"

"I'm going to use him," Clint said. "He's been playing in the same poker game with me for a few days, so I know where he'll be. I can use him to find the other man."

"What about Tom Colby?"

"I haven't seen him yet," Clint said. "I'll have to figure out a way to meet him without walking into his store."

"Well, he drinks at the Lulu Belle."

"The Lulu Belle?"

"Have you been there?"

"No," Clint said, "but I've seen it, and I heard about it just yesterday."

"From who?"

"A woman who came to my room to warn me."

He told Pike what had happened with Aurora Lane, leaving out the part about her spending the night in his bed.

"You're going to need somebody to watch your back," Pike said.

"I'll take care of it," Clint said. "I'll go to the Lulu Belle and deal with these men, and then see about meeting Tom Colby."

"I wish I could get out of this bed," Pike said.

"Do that and you'll do more harm than good," Clint said. "Just sit there and finish your sandwich."

"You've got to bring these again," Pike said. "And I'm going to start having my favorite restaurant in Washington make them."

"Be my guest," Clint said. "Do you have a gun in this room with you?"

"No," Pike said, "they wouldn't let me keep one."

"I'll smuggle one in to you tomorrow," Clint said. "We don't want to depend on the police to protect you."

"I don't know if anyone will come after me here," Pike said, "but a gun under my pillow would make me feel a lot better."

"I'll bring one," Clint promised. "Along with some more biscuits."

Clint headed for the door and Pike called out, "If you can only carry one, bring the biscuits."

SIXTEEN

Clint left the hospital, found a cab just letting some people off out front. It was a family, the parents walking a crying child—an eight- or nine-year-old girl, bleeding from the hand—into the building.

"What was that about?" Clint asked.

"Girl cut her hand playing with a knife," the driver said.

"Too bad," Clint said.

"Nah," the driver said, "that's how kids learn. Where ya headed, friend?"

Clint was stumped for a moment. Where was he headed this early in the day? Too early to go to either the Blue Owl or the Lulu Belle.

"I need to go to a farming equipment store," Clint said, "but I don't know where it is."

"Well," the driver said, "it's a big city and there are a few of them . . ."

"The one I want is owned by a guy named . . . Colby?" Clint asked. He didn't want anyone to know he was asking about Tom Colby, but he hadn't gotten the address from Pike, and didn't want to go back in.

"Tom Colby?"

"Is that him?"

"Well, he's a big man in town, sits on the town council, and he owns a farming equipment store."

"That's the one, then," Clint said.

"Hop in," the driver said. "That's on Grand Street. Let's go."

Clint climbed into the back of the cab, and they were off.

"It's just up the street," the driver called back a little while later.

"Just drop me here, then," Clint said.

"Don't you want me to drop you in front?"

"No," Clint said, "I want to make a quick stop first for some coffee."

"This café right here's got some good coffee," the driver said, pulling up in front.

"Good, thanks."

Clint got out and paid the man.

"Want me to stay around and wait?" the driver asked.

"No, that's okay," Clint said. "I'm good. Thanks."

"Just thought you might be a stranger and need someone to show you around."

"I've been in town for a few days now," Clint said. "Thanks."

The driver pulled away quickly, so there was no need for Clint to actually go into the café. Instead, he walked the rest of the way to Tom Colby's store.

Inside, Tom Colby was having a conversation with two men.

"The Secret Service man is out of the way," Jack Denim told Colby.

"I didn't want him out of the way," Colby said. "I wanted him dead."

"Jesus," the other man, Cole Roburt, said, "we shot him twice."

"Then you obviously should have shot him three times," Colby said.

"So whataya want us to do now?" Denim asked.

"I want you to finish the job," Colby said. "Get rid of him."

"When he gets out of the hospital?" Roburt asked.

"No," Colby said, "now, today, in the hospital!"

They were in the back of Colby's store, in the man's office, where nobody could see them together.

"Right in the hospital?" Denim asked.

"Yes, damn it!" Colby said. "Look, Ninger is getting nervous, and the only way to calm him down is to get rid of the man. You got it?"

"We got it," Roburt said, "but we'll have to watch the hospital, at least for a little while—"

"Look," Colby said, "do what you've got to do, but get it done, all right? I don't want to see either one of you until you can tell me he's dead."

"All right," Denim said.

"Yes, sir," Roburt said.

"Now get out," Colby said. "Use the back door and make sure nobody sees you."

The two men shuffled to the rear wall of the office and out the door. Colby immediately locked it behind them.

Goddamnit, he thought, if they didn't manage to get the job done, he was going to have to hire somebody who could. And he was going to have to spend more money. Real money, because he couldn't risk using any of the counterfeit stuff. The release of that money into the system had to be very closely monitored.

He was going to have to talk to his contact in the Saint Louis Police Department about this, see what they managed to learn from "Joshua Jones." He had to know if there was anybody else in Saint Louis that the man was working with.

He left his office and went back to work He had a new shipment of machine parts to inventory.

What are we gonna do?" Roburt asked Denim.

"I don't know about you," Denim said, "but I'm gonna play poker tonight."

"But the boss wants this man dead by tonight."

"Well, he's not out here doin' it, is he?" Denim asked. "We'll go and look at the hospital, see if this Secret Service guy is being watched."

"Watched?"

"Guarded."

"You think they got a guard on him?" Roburt asked. "How we gonna kill him, then?"

"I don't know," Denim said. "We'll see."

"We better get over there," Roburt said. "I gotta get to my game."

"Where are you gettin' all this money to play poker with?" Roburt asked.

Denim looked at him and asked, "Where do you think?"

Roburt grabbed his arm. "You're playin' with the counterfeit?"

"Why not?" Denim asked. "Nobody can tell the difference."

"If Colby ever finds out—"

"He won't," Denim said. "Not unless you tell him."

"I'm not gonna tell him," Roburt said.

"Then there's no problem," Denim said. "Let's get to that hospital."

SEVENTEEN

Clint stood outside the building for a little while, watching people go in and out. Several times he saw someone pull a buckboard up to a loading bay and offload some supplies. He'd seen several employees, but didn't know if any of them was Tom Colby.

There was no way he could go inside. Nobody would ever believe he was a farmer, looking for new equipment. He was going to have to depend on eyeballing Colby at the Lulu Belle, and he knew just who to press into service to help him do that.

He walked down the street a couple of blocks before stopping to find himself a cab, and then he told the driver to take him to the Lulu Belle.

The Lulu Belle was a large and lavish establishment, with a saloon and gambling hall, a theater, and a restaurant. It reminded him of the White Elephant Saloon in Fort Worth, Texas.

Because the restaurant opened early, so did the saloon, so he was able to go inside and order himself a beer at the bar.

"There ya go," the six-foot bartender said, setting it in front of him. "Ain't seen you in here before." The man had dark hair—lots of it, even sticking out from his collar and covering his forearms—and was in his mid-thirties.

Clint sipped the cold beer and said, "I've been in town for a while, and a friend of mine said I should check this place out."

"A friend?"

"Her name's Aurora Lane."

"Aurora, yeah," the bartender said. "She works here."

"Is she around?"

"She's probably in the building, but she won't be down here until later this evening."

"Ah," Clint said, "I suppose I'll just have to wait until then to see her."

"I could probably find her and tell her you're here."

"That'd be great," Clint said. "I could have a quiet beer with her before the rush."

"Yeah, she is a pretty popular gal," the bartender said. "Just wait here a minute and I'll see what I can do. Who should I tell her is here?"

"Clint," he said. "Clint Adams."

The bartender froze for a minute, then said, "Clint Adams?" as if he wasn't sure he'd heard correctly.

"That's right."

"The Gunsmith?"

"Right again."

"Well," the man said, "this is a pleasure." The bartender stuck his hand out. "My name is Blake."

"Nice to meet you, Blake."

"I'll, uh, go and find her for you."

"Thanks."

Blake moved around from behind the bar and went to the rear of the large room. Clint turned, beer in hand, and looked the room over. High chandeliers, mahogany and gold, the place could have been in the center of Portsmouth Square, in San Francisco.

There was literally no one else in the place, although he could hear the clink of glasses and dishes from the restaurant next door. There was a large open doorway that would lead to the theater and the restaurant.

He turned back to the bar and leaned over his beer.

Blake, the bartender, found Aurora in an office in the back, seated at a large oak desk, and asked, "What are you tryin' to do?"

"What do you mean?"

"Clint Adams is in at the bar, looking for you," Blake said. "When did you become friends with him?"

"Oh, that," she said. "Last night."

"Last night?"

"Relax, darling," she said, putting her hand on Blake's hand. "It's all part of a plan."

"What plan?" he asked. "We didn't discuss a plan."

"That's because I don't discuss my plans with you," she said.

"What? You don't think I'm smart enough to get it?" he demanded.

She scratched the back of his hand and said, "I don't keep you around for your brain, darling, remember? Just go out and tell Mr. Adams I'll be right out."

Blake pulled his hand away and started for the door.

"Wait," she said.

"What?"

"What did you tell him? About me, I mean?"

"Nothin'," he said. "Just that you worked here, and you probably wouldn't be down until evening."

"Okay, good."

"You didn't tell him you own the place?"

"I did not."

"Okay," he said, flapping his arms. "It's your plan."

"That's right, baby," she said. "It's my plan."

EIGHTEEN

Clint was half finished with his beer by the time Blake came back.

"Find her?" he asked.

"I did," Blake said. "She said she'll be out in a minute. You want me to top that off? On the house?"

"Sure," Clint said, pushing the mug across to the man. "Thanks."

Clint was working on the second beer when Aurora appeared. She was wearing a more modest gown than she'd had on when she came to his room. Still lots of flesh on display, but her shoulders were covered.

"Well, hello," she said. "I didn't expect to see you here this early."

"I wanted to come and see your operation."

"My operation?"

He smiled.

"You do own the place, don't you, Aurora?"

She looked at Blake, who threw his hands up.

"I didn't say a thing."

"Give me a glass of wine, will you, Blake?" she said.

"Sure."

"Yes," she said to Clint, "I own the place."

"Why play games?"

She shrugged.

"A girl's got to have a few secrets." She accepted a glass of red wine from the bartender.

"And the warning?"

"Oh, that was real," she said. "I did hear that. I can probably show you the three men later tonight."

"You think they'll come in again?"

"They've been here every night for four nights," she said. "Why would tonight be different?"

"Sounds like they're trying to drink up some courage," Clint said. "They might have left town."

"Without trying for you after four nights of talking about it?"

"Maybe there ain't enough booze in the place to give them enough courage," Blake said.

Aurora looked at him.

"Don't you have a puddle to clean off the other end of the bar?" she asked.

He frowned, but moved away.

"You talk to all your employees that way?" Clint asked. "Or just the ones who are in love with you?"

"Blake likes to be treated that way," Aurora said. "Trust me."

Clint looked over at the big man, shook his head. What makes a man enjoy it when a woman mistreats him? Or the other way around?

"What brings you here so early?" she asked. "Really?"

"Just getting the lay of the land," Clint said. "When those three men come in, where do they sit? Same table every time?"

"Yes," she said. "Come with me."

They took their drinks and he followed her to a table against the far wall, away from the gaming tables.

"Here," she said.

"Three, every time?"

"Every time."

He looked around, then looked back at the table.

"Okay," he said. "I'll be back in tonight."

"Good," she said. "I'll have the girls take special care of you."

"No," Clint said, "that's the one thing I don't want. Just have them ignore me."

"That'll be hard," she said, "but okay. Is there anything else I can do to help?"

"Yes," he said, "when I come in tonight, you can point out Tom Colby to me."

"Tom Colby?" She frowned. "He's on the town council. He will probably be the next mayor of Saint Louis. What's your business with him?"

"I don't really know that I have any business with him," Clint said. "But for now, I just need to know what he looks like."

"Well, okay," she said. "I can do that."

"Good. Does he come in every night?"

"A few nights a week," she said.

"Tonight?"

She shrugged.

"It's not a regular thing," she said. "He may be here, he may not."

"Well," he said, "I'll be here."

They walked back to the bar, and he set his empty mug on it.

"Come by about eight, if you can," she said. "We'll be in full swing by then."

"All right."

She walked him to the front door, stepped outside with him.

"How did you come to own such a place?" he asked. "It must have cost a fortune."

"It did," she said, "but I saved my pennies."

"A lot of pennies," he said, and walked away.

NINETEEN

When Aurora walked back into the saloon, Blake asked, "What's goin' on?"

"What do you mean?"

"Come on," he said. "You and the Gunsmith? What use do you have for a gunfighter?"

"I don't know," she said. "I guess I'm going to find out."

Denim and Roburt came out of the hospital.

"I told you," Denim said. "There's a guard."

"We gotta get rid of him."

"Right there in the hallway?"

"What else can we do?"

"We've got to see when they change the guard," Denim said. "You're gonna have to stay here and watch."

"Me?" Roburt asked. "Why me?"

"Because this is your fault."

"How is it my fault?" Roburt demanded.

"If you could shoot straight, we wouldn't be in this mess," Denim told him.

"Then why didn't you shoot him?"

"I should have," Denim said. "But it's too late now."

"So you kill him this time."

"I will," Denim said. "But you keep watch and see when they change the guard."

"And what are you gonna do?"

"Don't worry," Denim said. "I'll be back."

After Clint left the Lulu Belle, he went back to his hotel, then to the hospital to see Pike. The same policeman was seated by the door, and let him in with a nod.

"Back so soon?" Pike asked.

"Just a couple of questions," Clint said. "I found out that Aurora Lane owns the Lulu Belle."

"The woman who warned you?"

"That's right," Clint said. "If she owns that place, then she is a big business owner, just like Tom Colby is. Could she be involved?"

"With the counterfeiting?"

"Yes."

Pike shrugged.

"I suppose she could," Pike said. "Why? What did you tell her?"

"Nothing," Clint said. "I did ask her to point out Colby tonight, if he came into the Lulu Belle."

"There are three men in the Lulu Belle planning to kill you, and you're going to go there?"

"I'll have to take care of them," Clint said, "just so I don't have to worry about them."

"Well, good luck."

"Oh, yeah," Clint said. "Here." He took his Colt New Line from the back of his belt and held it out to Pike. "It's not very big, but it will do the job."

"Thanks." Pike put the gun under his pillow.

"I'll see you tomorrow." Clint started for the door, then stopped. "Do you know a girl named Izzy? Young? Pretty under a layer of dirt?"

"Izzy?" Pike thought. "No, never heard of her."

"Okay," Clint said. "Tomorrow."

Roburt saw Clint go into the hospital, but he saw a lot of people go in. He didn't know him so he didn't pay any attention to him. He was looking for a policeman in uniform who was coming to change places with the other one. So as Clint came out, he just lit a cigarette and ignored him.

TWENTY

When Clint came out of the hospital room, he saw Detective Donnelly standing there. The man in the uniform looked at Clint and shrugged.

"Mr. Adams," Donnelly said, "I hear you've been visiting our . . . friend."

"I'm trying to jog my memory," Clint said. "Also, he doesn't know anybody in town, so I'm just trying to help him out."

"I see. Do you think you'd have some time for me?"

"When?"

"Right now," Donnelly said. "I'll buy you a slice of pie or something."

"Coffee and pie sound good."

Donnelly exchanged a nod with the policeman, then said to Clint, "Let's go."

The detective took Clint to a café around the corner, another place that catered to the medical staff of the hospital.

"Good pie here?" Clint asked as they sat.

"I don't know," Donnelly said. "I've never had it here before."

A pretty young waitress came over and gave Donnelly a special smile.

"My friend wants to know if the pie is good here," Donnelly said to her.

"Pie's not very good here," she said, "except for the blueberry."

"What's so special about that one?" Donnelly asked.

She smiled at him broadly and said, "It's my favorite. I just can't eat it while I'm working 'cause it turns my teeth blue."

"I think you'd look real cute with blue teeth," Donnelly said. "Why don't you bring us two hunks of that blueberry pie, and a pot of coffee."

"Comin' right up, handsome."

She flounced away.

"Never had the pie here?" Clint asked.

"I've eaten here once or twice," Donnelly admitted, "just no pie."

"So what's this all about?"

"I've got something to tell you," Donnelly said. "And after I tell you, I'm hoping maybe you'll confide in me, as well."

"About what?"

"Just listen first."

"Okay."

They waited until the waitress served the two pieces of pie and coffee, and gave Donnelly a little hip bump before she left.

"She was right," Clint said. "The blueberry is pretty good."

Donnelly ignored his.

"Okay," he said, "I know that there are some factions inside my department who are . . . let's say, not exactly operating under the law."

"Is that right?"

"Yes, it is."

"How do you know that?"

"There's a little bit of a story behind that," Donnelly said.

"I guess we've got time."

Donnelly picked up his fork and cut off a hunk of pie. He put it in his mouth and chewed.

"Okay," he said. "Here it is."

TWENTY-ONE

"When I was a young policeman—five years ago, although it seems a lot longer—I discovered that many of the men I worked with were taking money from . . . outside influences."

"Influences?"

"Rich men, like Tom Colby," he said. "And others."

"But you didn't take money?"

"No," Donnelly said, "I did take it, but I did it because it was the only way I could remain a policeman."

"Why would you want to stay a policeman in that kind of a department?"

"I figured it was the only way I could effect change inside," Donnelly said, "by staying inside."

"And have you been able to?"

"No," Donnelly said, "and now a lot of the older men I looked up to ascended into power. Even the chief of police is . . . crooked."

"Why are you telling me this?" Clint asked. "Do you want me to help you clean up your department?"

"No, that's not it," Donnelly said. "See, I think that man in the hospital is a Secret Service agent. I think my chief knows he is, and passed that information on. That's why he was shot."

"And if he's a Secret Service agent," Clint asked, "why is he here?"

"The word inside my department is that there's a counterfeiter at work," Donnelly said. "Only they're not doing anything to find him."

"Why not?"

"Why else?" Donnelly asked. "They're all getting their piece . . . of the pie."

"And you?"

"Not a cent," Donnelly said. "Not since I was made detective two years ago."

"But?"

"But I've been doing my job, and not getting in anyone's way . . . until now."

"Why now?"

"Because if that man is a Secret Service agent, then this is the government we're talking about. I'm not going to take sides against my own country."

"And what do you want from me?"

"The truth," Donnelly said.

"And if I told you that Jones really is a government man?" Clint asked. "Then what?"

"I could help him," Donnelly said, "work with him, and you."

"Hey," Clint said, "I only came to Saint Louis to relax,

play some poker. I'm not involved in anything more than that."

"Maybe you weren't," Donnelly said, "but he asked for you. My guess is he recruited you."

Clint didn't reply. He ate the last bite of his pie, and sat back.

"I'm not asking you to tell me anything now," Donnelly said. "Think about it. Maybe talk it over with . . . whoever."

"I'll think about what you've said, Detective."

"I think you'll make the right decision, Mr. Adams," Donnelly said, "so you better start calling me Edward."

"Well, Edward," Clint said, standing, "I'll be in touch."

"I'm going to stay here a few more minutes," Donnelly said.

Clint looked over at the waitress, who was standing off to the side watching Donnelly.

"Good luck," Clint said, and left.

Clint stopped briefly outside the café, then continued walking. He had the feeling somebody was watching him, but as he walked away, he realized they were not watching him, they were watching the café.

Or maybe they were watching Detective Edward Donnelly.

"There goes Adams," one of the watchers said.

"Let's wait until he gets good and far away," the other man said.

"What if Donnelly comes right out?"

"He won't," the other man said. "He's sweet on a waitress inside."

"I wish we didn't have to do this," the first man said.

"Look, we got our orders," the other man said. "Let's just get it done."

They took out their guns and waited.

In front of the hospital, Cole Roburt was looking around, waiting for Denim to return. Another uniformed policeman had gone inside, and the first one had come out. He had seen others go in and out, but when Donnelly and Clint came out, Roburt didn't know either one of them.

Clint went around the corner, then stopped. He pressed his back against the wall and peered back around the corner. There were definitely two men across the street from the café. He had the feeling that Edward Donnelly was going to come walking out straight into an ambush.

TWENTY-TWO

Donnelly talked with the waitress for a few minutes, until she agreed to see him again later that night. He promised to come back at 8 p.m., when she'd finished work.

She smiled and waved at him, and he headed for the door.

The two men across the street saw him appear in the doorway.

"Now," the first man said.

"Why don't we wait 'til he comes—"

"Now, now!" the other man yelled.

"Wait—" the second man said, and that moment's hesitation cost them.

Clint came around the corner on the run toward the café. He saw the two men across the street shouting at each other, and knew he had a chance.

He pulled his gun and began firing . . .

* * *

Donnelly came out the front door, and before he knew it, lead was flying and Clint Adams was running down the street toward him.

And then the plate glass windows on either side of him shattered.

Clint's shots were pinpoint in their accuracy.

The bullets from his gun struck both men as they fired, and their shots went wild. He heard the glass shattering as he started across the street.

And then it got quiet . . .

Roburt didn't know what to do.

He heard the shots from around the corner, the commotion, didn't know what the hell was happening, and so he did the only thing he could think of.

He ran.

When Clint reached the other side of the street, the two gunmen were dead. He kicked their guns away, just to be sure.

He heard someone behind him, turned, and saw Donnelly running toward him with his gun out.

"What the hell—" Donnelly said.

"It was an ambush," Clint said.

"For me?"

"Well," Clint said, "they let me walk down the block without a shot."

"You saw them when you came out?"

"I did," Clint said, "and once I knew they weren't here for me . . ."

"You saved my life," Donnelly said.

"Do you know them?" Clint asked.

"Let's turn them over."

Both men were lying facedown. Clint turned one and Donnelly turned the other one.

"Shit!" he said.

"What?" Clint asked. "Do you know them?"

"They're both police," Donnelly said. "They're both from my department." He looked at Clint. "Why would they try to kill me in broad daylight?"

"Somebody's worried about you, Edward," Clint said. "Could your chief have sent them?"

"I suppose . . ." Donnelly was looking lost.

And then there was a scream from across the street.

"Now what?" Donnelly said.

They both ran back across the street to the café. The interior was strewn with broken glass, and in the center, somebody was lying on the floor.

"Aw damn . . ." Donnelly said.

It was the waitress. A bullet had caught her in the forehead, and her body had been further cut up by the flying glass. Some other customers were bleeding from cuts, as well. A doctor and two nurses were there from the hospital, and they were tending to the injured.

The doctor looked up at Clint and said, "We've sent for some proper equipment so we can treat them, but there was nothing we could do for her."

Clint nodded, looked over to where Donnelly was crouching by the dead girl.

"Her name was Lucy," he said.

Clint put his hand on the young man's shoulder.

"Come on, Edward," he said. "We have to go."

"Wha—"

"There's going to be more police here," Clint said, "and we don't know what they'll do when they get here."

"You mean—"

"You don't know who you can trust."

Donnelly stood up, glassy-eyed, and looked at Clint.

"Can I trust you, Mr. Adams?"

"Son," Clint said, "I have the feeling that right now, in this city, I'm the only one you can trust."

TWENTY-THREE

Clint pushed Donnelly along the street, the young man still slightly dazed.

"I've—I've never been shot at before," he confessed.

"You never get used to it," Clint told him.

"That poor girl."

"That's not your fault."

After leaving the café, Clint had run back across the street and gone through the pockets of the dead men. There was nothing there to indicate who might have sent them after Donnelly.

"Where—where are we going?" Donnelly asked.

"The hospital," Clint said.

"Why?"

"We've got to get Pi—Jones out of there before somebody tries to kill him."

"But . . . why—wha—"

"We can't think about that now," Clint said. "We just have to get you and Jones somewhere safe, so we can think."

"I can go back to Headquarters—"

"Not a good idea, son," Clint said. "If they tried to kill you in public like this, what do you think would stop them from killing you inside that building?"

"B-But . . . not all of them are—are crooked."

"The problem is," Clint said, "we don't know which is which. Until we can figure that out, you have to stay away from the police."

"B-But . . . I am the police."

"Maybe not so much anymore," Clint said.

When they reached the hospital, Clint checked out the street, didn't see anyone watching the building. He shoved the young detective up the steps to the front door and inside.

"What about the man on the door?" he asked as they went to the second floor.

"We'll have to see if he tries to stop us," Clint said.

"We—we can't kill him."

"Let's cross that bridge when we come to it," Clint suggested.

They reached the second floor and made their way down the hall. The policeman seated by the door looked up at them and just smiled. It was the same man Clint had given the sandwich to.

"What's going on, Detective?" he asked.

"We're just going to take Jones out for a meeting," Clint told him.

"Should I come along?"

"No," Clint said, "just stay here and watch the room. Make sure nobody goes in to hide there. We don't want to find a man with a gun in there when we get back."

"Okay."

They went into the room.

"Wha—" Pike started.

"Edward Donnelly," Clint said, "meet Jeremy Pike."

"Clint," Pike said, alarmed, "what are you do—"

"Two policemen just tried to kill Detective Donnelly," Clint said. "I'm thinking they might come for you next."

"Yes, but . . . my cover—"

"I think we three are in a position to trust each other, and nobody else," Clint said. "Donnelly suspected that you were a Secret Service agent, says he thinks somebody in his department gave him away."

"What can we—"

"Pike," Clint said, "we have to get you out of here. Where are your clothes?"

"In that closet."

"Get out of bed!" Clint ordered.

Pike got himself upright while Clint tossed his clothes onto the bed. Donnelly stood in the corner, still looking dazed.

"What's wrong with him?"

"He's never been shot at before," Clint said. "Plus, an innocent girl, a waitress, caught a stray bullet."

"Dead?" Pike asked while dressing.

"Yes."

The Secret Service man winced as he put his arm into his shirt, then buttoned it. He pulled on his trousers, then his suit jacket. When it came time to pull on his boots, he looked at Clint.

"I'm going to need help."

"Sit on the bed."

Clint helped the man pull on his boots. Pike stood up,

then turned to the bed and took the Colt New Line from beneath the pillow and tucked it into his belt.

"How does it look out front?" he asked.

"Clear," Clint said, "but I think we'll go out the back anyway."

"Okay."

"Edward," Clint said, then louder, "Edward!"

"Yes?"

"Come on, we're going."

"What about the man outside the door?" Pike asked.

"We told him we're taking you to a meeting, and we'll be back."

"And he believed that?"

"So far," Clint said. "Come on, let's go."

The three men left the room.

TWENTY-FOUR

Clint left Pike and Donnelly inside the back door of the hospital.

"I'm going to get a cab," he said. "Pike, you'll have to bring him out when I get back."

Pike looked at Donnelly, who still hadn't managed to come around.

"Yeah, okay."

Clint went outside, but had to go to the front of the hospital in order to find a cab. He caught one letting some people off, then recognized the driver as one he had used before.

"Hey," the driver said. "Visiting a friend again? Relative?"

"Can you keep quiet?" Clint asked.

"What?"

"For money?"

"Mister," the driver said, "I can do anything for money."

"Okay," Clint said, climbing into the back of the cab, "drive around to the back."

"The back of the hospital?"

"That's right."

"Hold on."

When they got around to the back, Clint said to the driver, "What's your name?"

"Danny."

He handed him a dollar and said, "Wait here, Danny, and there'll be more."

"I'll be right here, mister."

Clint got out of the cab and went to the back door. It was locked, so he banged on it. Pike opened it.

"Ready to go?" Clint asked,

"I guess so."

"What's wrong?"

"Donnelly is just not coming around," Pike said.

"Well, let's just take him someplace where we can work on him," Clint said.

Pike reached out and grabbed the front of Edward Donnelly's shirt, practically dragged him out of the building and into the cab.

"Where to?" Danny asked.

Clint looked at Pike.

"My hotel?" Clint asked.

Pike shook his head. "My hotel."

"Really?"

"They'll know where you're staying," Pike said, "and we can't go where he lives."

"Okay." He told Danny to take them to Pike's hotel, down near the docks.

"Down there? Really?" Danny asked. "I try to avoid that area."

"We'll make it worth your while."

"Hang on."

In front of the hotel, Clint paid the driver, who offered to wait.

"I don't know when we'll be back out," Clint said.

"From the looks of the place, it should be pretty soon," Danny said.

Clint thought a moment, then said, "Okay, yeah, wait here."

Danny smiled and saluted.

Pike let them into his room, which, if anything, smelled even worse than before. Donnelly didn't seem to notice.

"I'll open a window," Pike said.

The window overlooked an alley, so Clint doubted that would help—but it couldn't make things worse.

Donnelly sat down on the bed.

"Have you got any whiskey around?" Clint asked. "He needs a drink."

"I've got a bottle in the top drawer," Pike said. He went to the chest and got it, passed it to Clint.

"Here, Edward," Clint said, handing the bottle to the detective, "have a drink."

Donnelly took a big swig from it, then started coughing and choking.

"Another one," Clint insisted.

Donnelly took another drink, kept it down more easily.

"Come on, Edward," Clint said. "We need you."

"Yeah, yeah," Donnelly said. "Okay, I'm all right."

"Have you ever shot anyone?" Pike asked, easing himself down on the bed, wincing, holding his arm stiffly.

"No," Donnelly said.

"Well, that might have to change, too," the Secret Service man said.

"But . . . other lawmen?" Donnelly said. "I have to shoot other lawmen?"

"It may come to that," Clint said, "since they did try to shoot you."

"Yeah," Donnelly said, "they did, didn't they?" He looked at Clint and Pike. "So what do we do now?"

TWENTY-FIVE

"I think," Clint said, "that Edward should tell us as much as he knows about what's going on in his department," Clint said. "And then Pike, you should tell Edward everything you know."

"Everything?"

"Everything," Clint said, nodding, "about who you are and why you're here."

"Counterfeiting," Donnelly said, "right? That's what it's about?"

"How do you know that?"

"I've heard talk," Donnelly said. "I overheard my chief talking to some of the other policemen about it."

"What did he have to say?"

"That everybody would get a piece of the pie," Donnelly said, "as long as they cooperated."

"And they didn't approach you?" Pike asked.

"No," Donnelly said, "they know I'm honest . . . more or less."

"Start from the beginning, Edward," Clint said. "We'll listen."

Donnelly started talking . . .

"So you've taken money," Pike said, "but just so you can stay on the inside."

"Yes," Donnelly said.

"So the Saint Louis Police know about the counterfeiting."

"Yes."

"And haven't done anything about it."

"No."

"And, in fact," Clint said, "they might be helping."

"Exactly," Donnelly said. "So now you know what I know. What about you?"

"I'm Secret Service, sent here to track down whoever's running the counterfeiting ring," Pike said, "and whoever the counterfeiter is."

"And do you have any clues?"

"Tom Colby."

"Colby's involved?"

"It seems likely," Pike said.

"He's also likely to be the next mayor of Saint Louis," Donnelly said.

"I've heard that."

"I'm going to get a look at Colby tonight," Clint said. "Maybe I'll arrange to meet him."

"And you've got those three who are planning to kill you," Pike said. "You need someone to watch your back. Preferably someone who knows how to use a gun."

"I know how to use a gun!" Donnelly snapped. "I—I just have never been shot at before."

"Sorry," Pike said. "That wasn't a criticism of you. I just want Clint to be careful."

"I'll be careful," Clint said. "It's possible Aurora lied to me about that."

"Aurora?" Donnelly said. "Aurora Lane, who owns the Lulu Belle?"

"Yes," Clint said, "she told me she heard three men in her place planning to kill me."

"I wouldn't believe everything she says," Donnelly warned. "I'm pretty sure the chief is taking money from her, too."

"Do you think she's involved with the counterfeiting?" Clint asked.

"I don't know," Donnelly said. "I haven't heard anything about that specifically."

"Well," Clint said, "right now she's going to help me meet Colby. And I'll check out the three men, too, see if they're really after me."

"Are you going to ask them?" Pike asked.

"You know," Clint said, "maybe that's just what I'll do."

Roburt found Denim in the Blue Owl Saloon, standing at the bar.

"Not playing poker?"

Denim looked at him.

"The game will start a little later on," he said. "What the hell are you doing here? You're supposed to be watching the hospital."

"Somethin' happened."

"What?"

"I dunno," Roburt said. "There was a lot of shootin'

around the corner. I didn't know what to do, so I got the hell out of there."

"Because there was shootin' around the corner?" Denim asked. "Jesus, Roburt—"

"Look, you left me there alone," Roburt said. "I didn't know what to do."

"Well, great," Denim said. "Now we'll have to go back there and hope that Jones didn't leave while we were gone."

"Why would he leave?"

"I don't know!" Denim said. "He can't stay in the hospital forever. Come on! We gotta make sure—but if he is gone, you're gonna tell Colby about it, not me!"

TWENTY-SIX

Clint left Pike and Donnelly at Pike's hotel, warning them that if they left the building to get something to eat, they shouldn't go far.

"You're probably safer around the docks than anyplace else right now."

"If we go out to get something to eat, we'll bring it back here," Pike said.

"You should probably stay inside," Donnelly said. "You should still be in the hospital. I can get us something to eat."

"You fellas work it out between yourselves," Clint said. "I'll be back as soon as I can."

"I hope you come back with some information," Pike said. "If the police know I'm Secret Service, they'll be looking for both me and Donnelly. We're going to have to bring them down."

"I'll do my best," Clint said.

"And don't get killed!" Pike snapped as he left the room.

Clint had the waiting Danny take him to the Lulu Belle, where he dismissed him.

"Sure you don't want me to wait again?" Danny obviously thought he'd found himself as cash cow.

"No, that's okay," Clint said. "I may be here awhile."

Danny nodded and drove off.

As Clint entered the Lulu Belle, he felt the heat from the crush of bodies. He could hear the sounds of dice rolling, the roulette ball bouncing on the wheel, the wheel of fortune turning, and chips landing on chips as they were tossed into a pot.

He walked to the bar and managed to carve out a space for his body. He caught Blake the bartender's eye and waved him over.

"Beer," he said.

"Comin' up," Blake said.

Clint looked up and down the bar. None of the men drinking there paid any attention to him. He looked over his shoulder, trying to see the table the three men were supposed to be sitting at, but he couldn't see it through the crowd.

"Here ya go," Blake said.

"Thanks."

"Are you looking for Aurora?"

Clint sipped and said, "Eventually."

"I'll send word that you're here."

"Thanks."

True to her word, the saloon girls were passing him by, practically without a glance. She must have told them what he looked like and to avoid him. Either that or the bartender had pointed him out.

He thought about his poker game at the Blue Owl with Crane and Jack Denim. He was going to have to put in an appearance there, so nobody would wonder why he was missing. Either that or take Jack Denim out of the play. He didn't want to do that, however, without finding the second man, the one Denim was working with. Pike had said his name was Roburt. He had to get one of them to tell him who they were working for.

He turned and observed the room. He wondered if Colby was there somewhere. Maybe playing poker or blackjack or roulette.

He'd seen many men at the farm equipment store. Maybe one of them had been Colby—but he didn't see any faces that he found familiar.

He turned back to the bar and leaned over his beer.

After a few moments, the smell of perfume cut through the scent of smoke and sweat and beer. He turned to see Aurora smiling at him.

"You made it."

"I'm over an hour late."

"But you made it."

"Are they here?"

She nodded. "At the same table."

"And Colby?"

"He's here, too," she said. "Playing blackjack."

Clint frowned. Perhaps if he had been there earlier, he could have dealt with the three men without Colby being present. If he tried now, there might be a ruckus, and that would alert Colby to his presence.

"What are you going to do?"

"First," Clint said, "I want to see Colby. I'll worry about the other three later."

"Then come with me," Aurora said, sliding her arm through his. "We'll walk around."

"Let me get another beer," Clint said, "for appearance' sake."

Aurora signaled to Blake to bring Clint a full mug of beer. Once he had it, she said, "Let's walk."

They walked around the saloon floor for a few minutes, trying not to attract anyone's attention, before she finally stopped and, with a nod of her head, said, "He's over here. At the blackjack table."

He looked. There were four men playing blackjack, their backs to him. They were in the middle of a hand, and as he watched, all four men busted out.

"Which seat?"

"The one on the end," she said. "He always plays on the end."

"He's at the mercy of everybody else's draw that way," Clint said, shaking his head. "He should be sitting in the first chair."

"You obviously know the game."

"I prefer playing poker, myself," Clint said, "but yes, I know it."

"Well, I've tried to tell him the same thing," she said helplessly, "but he's got it in his head that it's his lucky seat."

"Well," he said, "that's the one thing that trumps logic in a gambler."

"What's that?" she asked.

"Superstition."

TWENTY-SEVEN

Clint asked Aurora to leave him alone for a few moments, so he could observe Colby without being noticed.

"I'll see you later," she said, and moved away into the crowd.

Clint used the next fifteen minutes or so to watch Colby, who seemed to play blackjack purely by instinct rather than logic. He didn't let what the players before him drew affect his actions. He also seemed to be in control of his emotions. By watching his face, you would never be able to tell if he had won or lost a hand. It told Clint a lot about the man himself.

Colby was in his forties, a wide-shouldered man who would probably be six feet when he stood up.

After a while, Clint felt he needed to move on, so as not to attract attention. So he continued to move about the room until he was able to see the table with the three men Aurora had told him about.

They looked like trail bums, all in their thirties, all

wearing six-guns and holsters, all drinking beer. They were loud, which explained how Aurora might have been able to overhear them. But wouldn't they have seen her standing close by them? She was a beautiful woman. It would be hard for her to go unnoticed by three young men.

From where he stood, though, he could hear the men bragging to each other about their sexual conquests. Wouldn't others have heard them talking about killing the Gunsmith?

By a stroke of luck, at that moment two men stood up and left their table, which was very near to the table where the three men were slapping each other on the backs. Clint moved quickly and sat down.

"A drink, handsome?" a saloon girl asked. Even if instructed to leave him alone, the girls still had to do their job.

"A beer."

"Comin' up."

He didn't know if any of the men knew what he looked like. It would be interesting if they did. However, they were still too busy bragging about themselves to look over at him.

The saloon girl brought him his beer, and as she passed the other table, one of the men reached out and grabbed her around the waist.

"Hey, girlie," he said, "why don't you take us all upstairs and tell us who's the best, huh?"

"Let go!" she snapped. "I've got work to do."

"That's what we're tellin' ya," one of the others said, "we want ya to work—on us."

"I'm not a whore!" she said.

"Who ya kiddin'?" the third man said. "All you girls are whores."

Even though the first man still had her by the waist, she

reached out and slapped the third man in the face. His face immediately turned red—both from the slap and from anger. He stood and grabbed her wrist.

"You're hurting me!" she cried.

"I'll do worse than that—" he said, raising his other hand to strike her. But by then Clint was there. When he saw that there was no security coming to her aid, he moved.

He caught the man's upraised hand and said, "Not today, friend."

The man yanked his arm from Clint's grasp. Clint ignored him and looked at the first man.

"Let her go."

"I'll let her go," the man said, releasing her, "but only so I can kill you."

The girl staggered back as he released her.

"Go on," Clint told her.

"Thanks, Mr.—" she said.

"Adams," he told her. "Clint Adams."

The three men stiffened when they heard the name.

"Thanks, Mr. Adams," she said, and moved away.

Clint looked at the first man.

"Still want to kill me?"

"H-Hey, look," the man said, "we was only h-havin' some fun—"

"I like fun," Clint said. "You mind if I get my beer and join you?"

"Uh, s-sure," the man said, "w-why not?"

"Thanks."

Clint collected his beer from his table, then pulled out the fourth chair and joined the three men, who were all now exhibiting signs of nervousness. One of them was blinking very rapidly.

"Now you fellas know my name," Clint said. "What are yours?"

"Um, I'm Briggs," the first man said.

"Turner," the blinker said.

The third man was the one the girl had slapped.

"I'm Evans."

"Well, what kind of fun were you boys having?" Clint asked.

"Ah, you know," Briggs said. "Just talkin' . . . braggin' . . ."

"Braggin', huh?" Clint asked. "You know, I heard there were some men in this saloon who were bragging about killing me. Was that you, boys?"

They all looked stricken and stared at each other, speechless.

TWENTY-EIGHT

"You boys don't have to be nervous," Clint said. "Lots of men plan to kill me. Some of them even try."

"Mr. Adams," Briggs said, "w-we never—"

"Oh, I know," Clint said, "you boys were just talking . . . bragging . . ."

"Well, uh, yeah . . ." Briggs said.

"But I just want you all to know," Clint said, "that if you did want to give it a try, I'd be happy to accommodate you out in the street."

"Uh, nossir!" Evans said. "We, uh, wouldn't wanna do that. Would we, boys?"

"Not at all!" Turner said, blinking rapidly. He looked as if he was about to cry.

"Well, that's good, then," Clint said. "I'll just leave you fellas to continue having fun."

He started to get up, then stopped.

"Oh, one more thing."

"Yessir?" Briggs asked.

"If it should occur to you to try to shoot me in the back? I wouldn't take too kindly to that."

"Oh, nossir!" Turner said. "We wouldn't try that."

"In fact," Evans said, "we was just talkin' about leavin' town."

"Oh, really? When?"

"Right now!" Briggs said. "We wasn't even gonna finish our drinks."

"Oh, that's silly," Clint said. "Your horses might break their legs out there in the dark." He slapped Briggs on the back, making the man jump. "Morning is soon enough. Just finish your drinks and turn in so you can get an early start."

"Uh," Evans said, "okay, we'll do that."

"'Night, boys."

Clint walked away, went back to the bar. Just moments later he saw all three men hurry out the batwing doors.

"'Nother beer?" Blake asked.

"Yup."

The bartender placed it in front of Clint.

"What'd you say to those boys?"

"I gave them some good advice," Clint said.

"Musta been really good advice," Blake said. "They about ran out of here."

Aurora appeared at his elbow, smiling.

"Looks like you handled that quietly."

"Luckily," he said. "Is Colby still here?"

"No," she said, "he lost some money, and left."

"That's okay," Clint said. "I know what he looks like."

"You didn't want to meet him?"

"Not tonight," Clint said. "Just wanted to spot him."

"So what are your plans for the rest of the night?" she asked.

"Why? What did you have in mind?"

"Just thought I might show you my rooms upstairs," she said, sliding her arm through his.

He thought about Pike and Donnelly waiting for him in the flophouse hotel, but they were prepared to take care of themselves. Maybe he could find out what was really on Aurora Lane's mind.

"Well," he said, "lead the way."

Aurora got a bottle of wine from Blake and then led Clint to the stairs. They went up to the second level, where she unlocked a door with a key. She tried to let him go in before her, but he said, "Ladies first."

"Do you think there's someone inside waiting to . . . what? Hit you over the head, or something?" she asked. "You're a careful man."

"A careful man who's still alive," he said, "despite all the odds."

Tom Colby, while sitting at the blackjack table, heard the murmurs in the crowd that the Gunsmith was present in the saloon. This surprised him because he'd heard, earlier in the week, that Clint Adams was around, but the word he got was that the man was playing poker down by the docks, in the Blue Owl Saloon.

What was the Gunsmith doing in the Lulu Belle, then? The opposite of slumming?

Although he didn't know that Clint Adams had been watching him earlier, he became aware of what was happening at a table of three loud men when Clint Adams interceded on behalf of one of the saloon girls. Adams sat with the three men—who seemed appropriately nervous—and

Colby—who had lost his stake for the night—took the opportunity to leave the saloon at that point.

There was much too much going on in the life of Tom Colby for him to be comfortable with the presence of the Gunsmith, not only in Saint Louis, but in the Lulu Belle.

He was going to have to have somebody look into that for him.

TWENTY-NINE

Aurora opened the wine, but did not get around to pouring it.

Once Clint was sure no one was going to leap out of the closet or from beneath the bed with a gun, he moved in behind the beautiful woman and slid his arms around her while she worked on the bottle.

"Mmm," she said as he pressed his crotch against her butt, "seems to me you're interested in something other than wine."

"I'm actually interested," he said into her ear, "in why you really came to see me in my room, pretending to be a saloon girl."

He kissed her neck, and she set the wine bottle down as his hands came up to cup her breasts.

"Ummm," she said, "what makes you think I wanted anything more than I got?"

"Because you're a smart woman," he said. "A smart

businesswoman. I don't think you really ever have only one single reason for anything that you do."

She turned in his arms then and pressed her mouth against his.

"Can we talk about this later?" she asked.

"Definitely."

When Colby got home, his wife greeted him at the door with a drink.

"How did you do?"

"I lost my stake," he said.

Colby was in his mid-forties. His wife, Ingrid, was ten years younger. They were a good fit because, while they had differing interests, they supported each other.

"I'm always impressed that you can lose your stake and come home," she said. "Most men would lose their stake and stay for more. Or waste more money on a whore."

"I gamble the way I run my business," he told her. "You know that."

She kissed him and said, "And I also know that I'm your whore, so you don't need another."

He snaked one hand around her to cup her firm butt, and kissed her.

"You're right about that, my love."

Arm in arm, they took their drinks and walked to their bedroom.

Clint took his time with Aurora.

He undressed her slowly, kissing each inch of skin that he exposed. By the time he had her naked, she was quivering, and wet. But he still went slowly.

He eased her down on the bed, then stood next to it and

removed his own clothes. As she reached for his hard penis, he slapped her hand away and said, "Not yet."

She pouted and reached again, but this time he backed out of her reach.

"Are you going to tease me?"

"Oh yes," he said.

He moved to the bed and ran his hands down her body. Those nipples grew turgid, and seemed to get darker. He circled them with his fingers, then ran his left hand down her body until he was cupping her pubic thatch. He could feel the heat from it on his palm, and knew if he probed with a finger, he'd feel her wetness. But he put that off . . .

"Come on, come on," she said, "please . . ."

"Just relax, Aurora," he said. "You're going to like this . . ."

When they reached their bedroom, Tom Colby and his wife, Ingrid, put their drinks down and slowly began to remove their clothes.

"Did anything else interesting happen tonight?" she asked.

"Yes," Colby said, "the Gunsmith was in the Lulu Belle."

"Is that significant?" she asked.

"I'm not sure," he said, "but I'm going to have to find out."

"Well," she said, naked now, "can you do that tomorrow?"

He eyed her long, sleek body, the small, hard breasts with their small pink nipples, and her smooth skin, and said, "Of course," reaching for her . . .

Clint spread Aurora's sleek legs and crouched between them. He kissed her inner thighs, licked them, came tantalizingly close to her pubic area, but kept skirting it, tickling the outer hairs, stroking her belly and her thighs, breathing on the area until it was good and hot, and then finally, probing through the hairs with his tongue. She gasped when the tip of his tongue touched her wetness. He lovingly stroked her wet slit with his tongue, enjoying the tart taste of her, reached up to cup her breasts at the same time.

She began to buck beneath him, saying, "Please, please . . ."

He kissed her vagina and said to her, "We're just getting started."

THIRTY

Ingrid Colby was a beautiful woman. And she loved her husband. He provided very well for her, allowed her to spend money without his approval. She was able to buy whatever she wanted, which was why she allowed him to do what he wanted when they were in bed together.

Colby loved her, but for some reason he could not perform in bed if she was looking at him. For that reason, he usually took her from behind. Once she was on her hands and knees in front of him, and he was looking at her fine ass, his cock quickly rose and hardened.

He reached between her thighs now, to finger her pussy until she was good and wet, and then slid his hard cock between her thighs, up into her.

The headboard slammed into the wall as he fucked her brutally that way . . .

Denim and Roburt stopped outside their boss's house, hesitating.

"What are you gonna tell him?" Roburt asked.

"I don't know," Denim said. "We can tell him that the Secret Service man is gone from the hospital, but if we tell him why, he'll kill you."

"Kill me?"

"Well, you left the hospital and let him get away."

"You can explain it to him, then."

Roburt studied the house, saw the light burning in what he knew was the bedroom.

"He just got home," he said. "We better give him some time to . . . do whatever he's doin'."

"With a wife who looks like his?" Denim asked. "I think we know what he's doin'."

"Then we better definitely give him some time . . ."

Aurora Lane was beating on the mattress with her fists as Clint licked and sucked her until the sheet beneath them was soaked with her juices. Only then did he mount her and drive his throbbing cock home.

She screamed as he pierced her, then wrapped her legs around him as he began to drive into her.

"Oh God, yesssss!" she screamed.

Tom Colby slapped his wife's ass until the skin was burning red. Only then did he explode into her, enjoying her screams of pleasure and pain combined . . .

"Did you hear that?" Roburt asked Denim.

"I sure did."

They were seated on the steps of the front porch.

"You think they're done?" Roburt asked.

"Sure sounded like it," Denim said. "A woman don't scream like that when she's just gettin' started."

"Should we knock?"

"Not yet," Denim said. "We better still give them some time to, you know, recover."

"Yeah."

Inside, Colby and his wife lay side by side on the bed, getting their breath back.

Ingrid's ass was stinging badly, but she would ease the pain by spending an obscene amount of money tomorrow.

"Did Roburt or Denim come by tonight?" he asked.

"No," she said, "why? Were they supposed to?"

"I gave them a job to do," he said. "If they didn't do it, I'm going to have to kill them."

"You can't kill them yourself, dear," she said. "You have a position in this town to maintain."

"You're right," he said. "I'll have them killed."

"What were they supposed to do?"

"Kill somebody."

"That sounds like a lot of killing," she said.

"It's necessary."

He stood up, went to the dresser, and got both their drinks. He came back and handed Ingrid her wineglass as she sat up in bed. She had beautiful skin.

"Who is it?" she asked. "The intended victim, I mean."

"A Secret Service agent."

That got her attention.

"Are you sure?"

"I don't know his name," he said, "but I'm sure enough to have him killed."

"Why didn't you have him killed before this?"

"They were supposed to kill him," he said, "but they only put him in the hospital. I was giving them a second chance."

"You don't usually give second chances, darling," she said, sipping her wine.

"I know," he said. "I was being unusually generous." He drained his wine and looked into the empty glass. "It won't happen again."

THIRTY-ONE

"Oh my God," Aurora said, "were you trying to kill me?"

Clint sat up in bed and said, "I was trying to make you happy."

"Well," she said, "you did that! My body is still shaking."

"Good," he said. "I'd hate to think all that effort went to waste."

"Oh?" she said. "It was an effort to make love to me?"

"No," he said, "it was a pleasure to make love to you. But now it's time to talk."

"Well," she said, "if you want to talk, you better put some pants on. I can't concentrate."

"Okay," he said, "and you better put on a robe."

"Or," she said, "we could take a bath together."

"I think we both know where that'll lead," he said, "and I have to . . . get back."

"Back?"

"To my hotel."

"Ah, well . . ." She stood up, walked to a changing screen against one wall, grabbed a robe off it, and pulled it on.

"Is this better?" she asked, tightening the belt.

"Much," he said, pulling on his trousers. "How about this?"

"Pull on your shirt, too, just to be sure," she suggested.

"Okay, then I might as well just get dressed."

She sat on the bed and watched as he pulled on his boots and donned his shirt. His gun belt was hanging on the bedpost, but he left it there for the moment.

"Now I suppose you want to talk," she said.

"Yes."

She folded her arms.

"Ask your questions."

"Why did you come to see me?"

"I did hear those men talking about you," she said, "and I did check all the hotels to see where you were."

"Why?"

"I wanted to meet you."

"Again, why?"

"Well, I'd heard so much about you and I was curious." She smiled at him slyly. "By the way, everything I heard was true, and more."

"Aurora . . ."

"Oh, all right," she said. "I thought you might be able to help me."

"Help you with what?"

"Getting away from my partner."

"You have a partner in the saloon?"

"Yes."

"Who is it?"

She made a face and said, "Tom Colby."

"Colby. Is he a full partner?"

"Actually," she said, "he's more of an investor than a partner."

"But?"

"But he's trying to push his way in, and I don't know how to keep him out."

"How hard is he pushing?"

"Well, lately, not as hard as he was. Something else has his attention."

"And I think I know what it is," Clint said.

"What?"

"I can't tell you," he said, "but if I take care of it, he won't bother you anymore."

"That sounds good to me."

"As long as you're not in business with him in any other way."

"What? No, I'm not. What do you mean?"

He stared at her.

"You mean this other thing you can't tell me about?" she asked. "I don't know what you're talking about, Clint."

"That's good, Aurora," he said. "That's very good. Because I wouldn't want Colby to know I'm coming for him."

"Well," she said, "he's not going to hear it from me."

He hoped she was telling the truth.

When Clint got back to the flophouse hotel, he found Pike and Donnelly sitting quietly, one on a rickety chair, the other on the bed.

"We can't stay here," Donnelly said. "It's too small and it stinks."

"I forgot how much it stinks," Pike said, "but after being in the hospital, where it smelled clean, this is pretty bad."

"Okay," Clint said, "I suppose we can move the two of you to my hotel. I'll smuggle you in the back door."

"Good," Donnelly said, and both men stood up.

"Gather your things, Pike," Clint said.

"I don't have much," Pike said.

"Don't forget those bills."

"Right."

"What bills?" Donnelly asked.

"Might as well show him," Clint said.

Pike pulled out the drawer and showed Detective Donnelly the funny-money hundred-dollar bills.

"Counterfeit?" Donnelly asked, picking one up.

"Yes."

He held the bill up to the lamp on the wall.

"It's a good job," Donnelly said, "except for this green line."

"You've got a good eye," Pike said as Donnelly handed the bill back.

"Only hundreds?" Donnelly asked.

"No, whoever it is, he's also doing fifties."

"Do you know who's making them?"

"We have an idea who's passing them," Pike said.

"And maybe who's backing the play," Clint said.

"But not exactly who's making them."

"Who's the backer?" Donnelly asked.

"Looks like Tom Colby," Pike said.

"You got proof?"

"Not yet," Pike said. "I was working on that when I got attacked."

"I see."

"Ready?" Clint asked.

Pike held up a small carpetbag and said, "I'm ready. Let's get out of here."

THIRTY-TWO

Tom Colby came down the next morning and found breakfast on the dining room table. The cook, Mrs. Preston, was puttering around the kitchen. His wife, Ingrid, was seated at the table, drinking tea.

"Good morning," he said.

"Morning. Who was that at the door last night?" Ingrid asked. "I was asleep by the time you came back up."

He sat down, and Mrs. Preston appeared with a cup and a pot of coffee. She filled the cup and returned to the kitchen. Colby and his wife both had bacon and eggs in front of them.

"It was Denim and Roburt."

"Did they do the job?"

"They did not."

"My my," she said, buttering a piece of toast. "You didn't, uh—"

"Kill them? No, I didn't," he said, "but I still may have it done."

"What happened?"

"They lost the Secret Service man."

"But . . . he was in the hospital."

"That's right," he said, "he *was*, but apparently he's not anymore."

"Good God," she said, "what are you going to do?"

"Find him," Colby said. "I'm going to find him right after breakfast."

He picked up his fork, and they stopped talking.

Clint woke the next morning to the sound of snoring. Because Pike was injured, he had given the man his bed. He and Donnelly were sleeping on the floor, at opposite ends of the room.

He sat up and squinted at the sunlight coming in the window.

"I need food," Donnelly said.

"Didn't you fellas eat last night?"

"Yes," Donnelly said, "but that was last night. I need some food this morning."

"Well, let's see what we can do about that."

They both stood up and looked over at Pike. All the activity last night seemed to have taken a lot out of him. His pallor was bad, and he was sleeping soundly.

"We could go down to the dining room," Clint said, "and bring something back for him. Will anyone there recognize you?"

"I'm not well known, Mr. Adams," Donnelly said. "Unless a policeman walks in, I should be okay. Besides, if I'm correct, people will be looking at you, won't they?"

"That's true."

"Then let's go."

They eased out of the room without waking Pike.

Despite his rumpled clothes—which he had slept in—Donnelly was able to go unnoticed in the dining room. Clint got them a small table off to one side, and they each ordered steak and eggs.

"See anybody you know?" Clint asked.

"No," Donnelly said, "but I can't afford to eat here, and most of the men I know can't either."

"What about your chief?"

"He might be the only one."

"You got any thoughts about what to do today?"

"I was thinking of talking to my chief," he said. "I know what you said yesterday, but I don't really think they'd kill me right in the building."

"You might be right."

"By now, whoever sent those two after me knows they missed," Donnelly said. "I'd like to see the chief's face when I walk into his office."

"That sounds like it might be a good idea," Clint said, "but how about if I go with you?"

"Oh, they definitely wouldn't kill me in front of you."

"I think you're right."

"Unless . . ."

"Unless what?"

Donnelly shrugged and said, "Unless they kill you, too."

Clint put a hunk of steak in his mouth and chewed with gusto.

THIRTY-THREE

Clint and Donnelly decided to play it brazenly. The young detective insisted he'd be able to tell if the chief had sent the two men to kill him just by his reaction.

"Are you sure?" Clint asked.

"His face hides nothing," Donnelly said. "He'd make a terrible poker player."

Donnelly's comment reminded Clint of his poker game at the Blue Owl. He wondered if Jack Denim was still playing. That should probably be the next stop for him and Donnelly. Grab Denim and squeeze something out of him. And then Tom Colby.

It promised to be a busy day.

They brought some food back for Pike, who was awake, and they told him the plan while he ate.

"I should go with you," Pike said. "You could be walking into a den of vipers."

"We could be," Donnelly said, "but I know there are still a lot of honest men in the department."

"Well," Pike said, "I hope for your sakes, you're right."

When Clint and Donnelly reached the front steps of Police Headquarters, several policemen were coming down toward them. They all nodded to Donnelly, who returned the nod.

"See what I mean?" he asked.

"No hint of surprise."

"Honest men."

They went up the steps and entered the building. There was a different man behind the desk than the last time Clint was there, but this one also had three stripes.

"Hey, Sarge," Donnelly said.

"Donnelly," the man said. "Where the hell have you been? The chief's been lookin' for you."

"Well, that's good, because I'm here to see him."

"Who's this?" the man asked.

"He's with me," Donnelly said.

"Hey, wait—" the sergeant started, but Donnelly hurriedly moved past the desk with Clint in tow.

"Let's go straight to his office," Donnelly said. "I don't want to give anybody a chance to tell him I'm here."

"I'm with you."

They went down a hallway and Donnelly finally stopped in front of a door.

"Ready?" Donnelly asked Clint.

"As long as he doesn't start shooting as soon as he sees you," Clint said.

"He may be taking money," Donnelly said, "and he may be involved with the counterfeiters, but I don't think he's a killer."

He reached for the doorknob, turned it, and shoved the door open. A florid-faced man looked up, and his face got even redder.

"Donnelly! Goddamnit, don't you knock?"

"I was told you wanted to see me right away, Chief."

"I do," the chief said. "Who's this?"

"Chief, meet Clint Adams."

"The Gunsmith?" the chief asked. "What the hell are you doin' in Saint Louis?"

"I was playing poker," Clint said.

"And?"

"The man in the hospital asked for him, Chief," Donnelly said. "So I found him."

"The man in the hospital is gone!" the chief snapped. "And two of our men were shot right around the corner from the hospital."

"We know about that, Chief."

"You know?" the chief asked. "What the hell are you talkin' about, you know? And where've you been anyway? You never came back here last night."

"We know," Donnelly said, "because we shot them."

"You mean—" the chief started, then stopped. He frowned, seemed to give the matter some thought, then said, "Maybe you better tell me what the hell you're talkin' about, from the beginning."

"Can we sit?" Donnelly asked. "This may take a while . . ."

THIRTY-FOUR

Clint remained silent, allowed Donnelly to tell the chief whatever he felt entitled to. In Clint's opinion, the chief didn't know anything about the two dead policemen trying to kill Donnelly. In fact, the man's face grew more and more perplexed as Donnelly spoke. Clint felt the young detective was right; this man would have made a lousy poker player.

When Donnelly had finished talking, the chief sat back in his chair and took the time to light a cigar.

"That is the craziest story I've heard in a long time," the chief finally said.

"Well, it's true," Donnelly said.

The chief looked at Clint. The air was now almost blue with cigar smoke.

"And you corroborate this story, Mr. Adams?" the man asked.

"I do."

The chief frowned.

"Shut that door!" he said to Donnelly.

Donnelly stood up and closed the door, wondering if the chief would have shot him in the back if Clint hadn't been there. No, he was sure his boss didn't know anything about the attempt on his life. That much he felt sure of.

He turned and sat back down.

"The two dead men were named Linwood and Downing. They worked as partners on foot patrol. I know they had their hands out to the merchants, but that kind of thing doesn't bother me."

"It doesn't?" Clint asked.

"Not in the larger scheme of things," the chief said. "See, I know there's a counterfeiter at work in town, and I know he's got somebody in my department."

"Who?" Donnelly asked.

"That, I don't know," the chief said, "but I'm guessing he's the one who sent Linwood and Downing after you." He looked at Clint. "It's too bad we can't ask one of them."

"Yes," Clint said, "too bad."

"Who do you have working on it?" Donnelly asked.

"As of today," the chief said, "I have you."

"Me? I mean, who's been working on it up to now?"

"Up to now," the chief said, "I haven't known who I can trust."

"And now you can trust me?"

"Well," the chief said, "somebody did try to kill you. You must be getting too close."

"To what?"

"The counterfeiters."

"If I am, I don't know it."

"You know the fella who was in the hospital is Secret Service. Work with him."

"He's in no condition to work on anything," Donnelly said.

"How do you know that?"

"Well . . . he was shot."

"And you know where he is?"

Donnelly didn't answer.

"Okay, forget that," the chief said, and pointed at Clint. "Work with him, then."

"I'm not a policeman," Clint said, "or a Secret Service man."

"But you're here with Donnelly," the chief said, "so you must be involved."

"Must I?"

"Look," the chief said, "this has been very frustrating for me, and now I see a way out."

"Me?" Donnelly said.

"You're a good detective," the chief said, "and you're the Gunsmith." As if that explained it all.

"Well," Clint said, "we do have some ideas."

"Don't tell me!" the chief said quickly.

"Why not?" Donnelly asked.

"If what you know gets out to the wrong people, I don't want you thinking they heard it from me. Got it?"

"I've got it," Donnelly said.

"Look," the chief said, "you're off the clock for this. You don't have any regular duties. Just work on this one case." The chief looked pleased with himself. "I've been waiting for the chance to say that to somebody."

"What's happening with the two dead men?" Clint asked. "I mean, how are you explaining that?"

"Right now they're at the undertaker's," the man said. "I've got another detective working on it."

"Who?" Donnelly asked.

"Callahan."

"He's stupid."

"I know," the chief said, "but I had the feeling I didn't want that case solved too quickly. Now I know why."

"So then, I'm not . . . in trouble."

"No," the chief said, "but you will be if you don't catch me a counterfeiter—and the traitor in my department."

"I'll do my best."

"I know you will, son," the chief said. "There's a promotion in it for you."

"What's in it for me?" Clint asked.

The chief looked at him and said, "Satisfaction."

When they got outside the building, they stopped at the base of the steps.

"What did you think of that?" Donnelly asked.

"I think you were right about him," Clint said. "He'd make a terrible poker player, but maybe he's a good chief of police."

"What makes you say that?"

"He recognizes that you're a good detective, doesn't he?"

"Well, yeah."

"And are you?" Clint asked. "A good detective, I mean."

"I am."

"Okay, then," Clint said, "let's prove it."

"How?"

"I know where to find one of the men who shot Pike," Clint said. "We can start with him. If he'll tell us who he's working for . . ."

"That would definitely be a step in the right direction."

"And failing that, we can just go and talk to Colby."

"They say he might be the next mayor."

"Well," Clint said, "not if he turns out to be a counterfeiter."

THIRTY-FIVE

As they entered the Blue Owl Saloon, Clint saw Crane the gambler at the poker table, with three new faces. No sign of Jack Denim.

"Damn," he said, "he's not here."

"Well, where is he?"

"I don't know," Clint said. "Let's get a beer, and then I'll ask."

They went to the bar and ordered two beers.

"Haven't seen you lately," the bartender said.

"I've been busy," Clint said. "Have you seen Jack Denim around?"

"Not for a while," the bar dog said. "Crane's had to find himself some new blood."

"Still winning?"

"Oh, yeah," the bartender said. "That hasn't changed."

Clint heard a chair scrape on the floor and looked over to see Crane standing up. He came walking over.

"Buy you a beer?" Clint asked.

"Sure," Crane said. "Where've you been?"

"I got caught up in something." The bartender handed the gambler a beer. "Have you seen Denim around?"

"No," Crane said. "He hasn't been back to the game either. Who's this?"

"This is Detective Edward Donnelly of the Saint Louis Police Department," Clint said.

"The police?" Crane said. "Are you under arrest?"

"No," Clint said, "we're working together."

"Doing what?"

"Right now," Clint said, "looking for Jack Denim."

"Well," Crane said, "he hasn't been around."

Clint exchanged a glance with Donnelly.

"Thanks for the beer," Crane said, and carried it back to the table.

"Colby next?" Donnelly said.

"Let's go and see Pike first," Clint said. "Maybe he's got some ideas."

"Sure, why not? This all started out as his assignment anyway."

They finished their beers, put down their mugs, and left the Blue Owl.

After Clint and Donnelly left the saloon, Henry Crane tossed his hand down and said, "Deal me out, boys. I got something to do."

He gathered up his money and left the saloon.

Jack Denim and Cole Roburt stood outside Police Headquarters.

"I don't like this Eastern crap," Roburt said. "I liked it better when there was just a sheriff."

"You like sheriffs?" Denim asked.

"No," Roburt said, "that ain't what I meant. Look, we gotta go in there?"

"No," Denim said, "we'll just wait here until our man comes out."

"And then what?"

"And then we'll take it from there," Denim said. "Just relax."

"How am I supposed to relax?" Roburt asked. "We don't get this done and Colby will kill us."

"He can't kill us both," Denim said. "In fact, he won't kill us at all. He gets other people to do his killin' for him—like us."

"So he'll have somebody else kill us, is that what you're sayin'?" Roburt asked. "That don't make me feel much better."

"Cole," Denim said, "just do what I tell you, and we'll be fine. You'll see."

"Yeah," Roburt muttered, "I'll see."

THIRTY-SIX

Back at Clint's Hotel, the Mayflower, they found Pike sitting up in bed.

"How are you doing?" Clint asked.

"I'm okay," Pike said. "Feeling a bit stronger. You fellas find out anything?"

"I'll let Detective Donnelly fill you in," Clint said.

He sat at the foot of the bed while Donnelly told Pike about their meeting with the police chief.

"And you believe him?" Pike asked afterward.

"Yeah," Donnelly said.

"We both do," Clint said.

"So nobody's looking for you," Pike said to Donnelly. "You can move around."

"Not exactly," Clint said. "Those two crooked lawmen did try to kill him. There's no telling when somebody might try again."

"So what's on your minds now?"

"Tom Colby," Clint said, "unless you have a better idea."

"You plan on bracing Colby?"

"Maybe shake him up a bit," Clint said, "see what he does."

"What do you think?" Donnelly asked.

"Sounds like a plan," Pike said. "Maybe I can come along."

"First let's see how fast you can get off the bed," Clint said.

Pike was still inching his way to the edge of the mattress when Clint said, "I think you better just stay there, Pike."

"Maybe I do need a few more days," Pike agreed.

"You got a gun?" Donnelly asked.

"Yes, Clint gave me one."

"Okay, then," the detective said. He looked at Clint. "Let's see if we can catch Colby at home."

"Does he have an office?"

Donnelly nodded.

"On Market Street," he said, "but he's hardly ever there. We're most likely to find him at home, with his wife."

"Do you know his wife?" Clint asked.

"I've seen her," Donnelly said, "which is how I know he'll probably be home. If I had a wife who looked like her, I'd stay home, too."

"Attractive?" Pike asked.

"Beautiful," Donnelly said, "and younger than him by about ten years."

"Let's go and see."

They caught a cab, and Donnelly directed the driver to Tom Colby's house, which was on a tree-lined residential street near Forest Park.

"This is serious money," Clint said.

"I told you," Donnelly said, "everybody's saying he's going to be the next mayor."

"Maybe we can put a crimp in his plans."

They approached the front door and Donnelly knocked. They had agreed that since he was the man with the badge, he would do the talking.

The door was opened by a middle-aged woman wearing an apron and a frown.

"What is it?" she asked.

"My name is Detective Donnelly, of the Saint Louis Police Department," the young detective said. "Are you the housekeeper?"

She shook her head and said, "Cook."

"Is Mr. Colby home?"

"He is," she said, but she didn't move.

"Could we see him, please?"

She looked at Clint, sniffed and said, "Wait here," then closed the door.

"I don't think she likes you," Donnelly said.

"I don't think she likes anybody."

When the door opened, the woman was standing there again.

"I would like to see your badge."

Donnelly took it out and showed it to her.

"And his?"

"He's not a policeman," Donnelly said, "but he's my colleague."

"I see." She seemed unsure about what to do, but finally said, "Well, come in."

They entered and waited while she closed the door and locked it.

"Mr. Colby will see you in his study. Follow me, please."

Clint wondered why all rich men had to have a room in their house, usually filled with books, that they either called their "office," their "library," or their "study."

They followed the cook down a hall to an open door, and into the study. It was larger than what most men would call an "office." The word "study" fit it much better. Three of the walls were covered with books. In the center of the room stood a large, oak desk with Tom Colby behind it.

"Mr. Colby, these are Detective Donnelly and . . ." She stopped, because she didn't know Clint's name.

"Clint Adams," Colby said, standing. "Welcome, gentlemen."

"You know who I am," Clint said.

"You're quite a famous man, Mr. Adams," Colby said. "I make it my business to know important people."

"Well, I don't know how important I am to anyone," Clint said.

"History, sir, history," Tom Colby said. "You will have a firm place in history."

"That's not what we're here about," Donnelly said, and Clint was glad he stepped in.

"Then what are you here about, Detective?" Colby asked.

"This."

Donnelly took one of the phony hundred-dollar bills out of his pocket.

"A hundred-dollar bill?" Colby asked, laughing. "I have a lot of them."

"Not like this one." Donnelly held it out.

Colby hesitated, then frowned, leaned forward, and took it from the detective. He studied it, held it to the light, then looked at them.

"This is counterfeit?"

"It is."

"It looks real."

"It looks very real," Donnelly said, "but I can tell."

"How?"

Donnelly held out his hand and Colby gave the bill back. Instead of showing Colby what made it phony, he put it away.

"I can tell," Donnelly said. "That's all that matters."

THIRTY-SEVEN

"That still doesn't explain what brought you here," Colby said.

"You're an important man in this city," Donnelly said. "As you just said, you make it your business to know everyone important."

"And?"

"I don't know how anyone could be counterfeiting," Donnelly said, "and passing the bills without you knowing about it."

Colby sat back.

"Normally, I would think you were right," he said, "but I don't know anything about this."

"But you could find out," Donnelly said.

"Are you asking me to help the police?" Colby asked. "To help you?"

"I am," Donnelly said. "Everyone says you're going to be the next mayor of Saint Louis. I would think you wouldn't want anyone flooding it with funny money."

"You have a point," Colby said. "What is it you think I can do?"

"You know a lot of people," Donnelly said. "Put the word out. Find out who's passing bills. Or who's making them. Just find out something that will help me."

Colby sat back in his chair and seemed to be considering the request.

"All right," he said. "I can do that much, I guess."

"Good," Donnelly said. "We'd appreciate it."

"But I wonder," Colby said. "If this is about counterfeiting, why isn't someone from the government approaching me?"

"There is a man here from the government," Donnelly said, "but he's been injured. We're keeping him somewhere safe until he recovers."

"I see. And I don't suppose you'd care to tell me who he is, or where he is?"

"That's not necessary for you to know, Mr. Colby," Donnelly said.

"I suppose not. Well, all right. First thing in the morning, I'll get the word out."

Donnelly and Clint stood up. Colby followed, and shook hands with both of them.

"What's your part in all this?" Colby asked Clint.

"I'm just here to keep Detective Donnelly alive," Clint said.

"Well," Colby said, "I suppose he couldn't have a better bodyguard than the Gunsmith, could he?"

THIRTY-EIGHT

As the cook was showing them to the door, another woman appeared. This one was tall, in her thirties, with honey-colored hair piled high on her head. She was beautiful. Obviously, this was Tom Colby's wife.

"That's all right, Mrs. Preston," she said. "I'll show them out."

"But the mister told me—"

"I'm telling you it's all right," the woman said. "Go back to the kitchen."

"Yes, ma'am."

The woman turned and walked away.

"We've needed a new manservant for some time," she told them. "Finding a good one is difficult."

"I'm sure," Clint said.

"Gentlemen," she said. "I'm Ingrid Colby."

"Mrs. Colby," Donnelly said. "It's a pleasure to meet you. I'm Detective Edward Donnelly."

She nodded to him, then looked at Clint.

"And you?"

"Clint Adams."

"Ah," she said, "the Gunsmith." He noticed her eyes were slate gray. He hadn't seen that color very often in a woman. It made her eyes look cold. "My husband must have been very excited to meet you."

"If he was," Clint said, "he hid it well."

She smiled.

"He hides his emotions well," she said. "It's very helpful in business. Believe me, he was excited."

"All right," Clint said. "I believe you."

"I must admit," she went on, "I'm getting kind of excited myself."

Just for a moment it looked as if her gray eyes grew warmer.

"I'm assuming you didn't come here to arrest my husband, Detective."

"You assume correctly, ma'am," he said. "We came to ask for his help."

"Well, since he's going to be our next mayor, I'm sure he agreed."

"He did."

"Good," she said. "I'll show you both to the door, then."

At the front door she opened it, allowed Donnelly to go through. Before Clint could follow, she took hold of his left sleeve.

"It was a pleasure to meet you, Mr. Adams," she said. "Perhaps we'll see each other again . . . soon."

He looked into her eyes.

"Perhaps," he said.

Definitely hotter.

* * *

Outside of the house, Donnelly said to Clint, "How do you think I did?"

"You did fine," Clint said. "He's guilty as sin."

"I think so, too," the detective said. "What do you think he'll do now?"

"He'll send somebody after you," Clint said. "After us. When he does, they'll lead us right back to him."

"If we survive," Donnelly pointed out.

"Well, yes, there is that."

Donnelly turned and looked over his shoulder at the house, then back at Clint.

"What do we do now?"

"We have to be somewhere they can find us," Clint said. "Someplace picked by us."

"Where should that be?"

"This is your city," Clint said. "You decide."

"Do you think we can count on Pike to help?"

"He'll help all he can," Clint said. "I'm sure of that. The question is, how much is he capable of?"

Ingrid Colby entered her husband's study. He was still seated behind the desk, thinking.

"How did that go?" she asked.

He stroked his chin.

"They asked for my help."

"That's good."

He looked at her. "Is it?"

"What's wrong?"

"I don't know," he said. "Something."

"Like what?"

"Like maybe they know I'm involved."

"How would they know that?"

"I don't know," he said. "It's just a feeling."

"Well," she said, "maybe we should act on that."

"How?"

"I might just know a way," Ingrid said thoughtfully.

THIRTY-NINE

When they got back to the Mayflower, Clint got a second room for Pike to use.

"What if they come after you?" Pike asked.

"That's what we want," Clint said. "If somebody comes after me, it's going to be because Colby sent them."

"We'll be right down the hall," Donnelly said. "This way you can continue to rest."

Clint and Donnelly offered to help Pike move down the hall, but the Secret Service man was able to walk on his own.

"Get on that bed," Clint said.

"I'm fine—"

"Just humor me," Clint said. "If something happens, you can get off the bed."

"Fine."

Pike got on the bed, boots and all.

"Okay," Clint said. "I'm going back to my room."

"I'm kind of hungry," Pike said.

"Actually, me, too," Donnelly said.

"Okay," Clint said, "we'll go downstairs and get something to eat. Pike, we'll bring you something."

"Why don't I come?" he asked. "I mean, we want them to find us, right?"

Clint and Donnelly exchanged a glance, and then Clint said, "Okay, but let's go right now."

"Good," Pike said, "because right now is when I'm hungry."

They settled into a table in the hotel dining room, which was just starting to fill with diners. Clint and Pike ordered steaks, while Donnelly ordered beef stew.

"You think this is going to work?" Pike asked. "Offering yourselves up as bait?"

"It'll work," Donnelly said, "as long as Tom Colby is guilty."

"If he's not," Clint said, "then we have to start over."

"From the beginning," Pike said, "which is where I started."

"You're the one who came up with Colby's name."

"I did," Pike said, "and I still think he's involved, but this is not the way we fulfill our assignments in the Secret Service, by becoming targets."

"Well, if this works," Donnelly said, "maybe it should be."

When the waiter came with their food, they were all hungry enough to stop talking and dig in.

They were eating pie and having coffee when Donnelly looked up and said, "Uh-oh."

Clint looked up at the door and saw what he was talking about.

"What is it?" Pike asked.

"The woman at the door," Donnelly said.

"What about her?" Pike asked. "She's beautiful."

"She's also Ingrid Colby," Clint explained. "Tom Colby's wife."

Ingrid Colby was wearing a gray skirt and jacket, and calfskin boots.

"I wonder what she wants here," Pike asked.

"I guess we're about to find out," Donnelly said. "She's on her way over here."

All three men stood as she reached their table, Pike a little bent over.

"Please, gentlemen," she said. "Sit."

They all did.

"And who is this?" she asked.

"Mrs. Colby," Clint introduced, "this is our friend Joshua Jones."

"Mrs. Colby," Pike said.

"Mr. Jones," she replied. "I hope you and Detective Donnelly won't hold it against me if I take Mr. Adams away for a while."

"Uh, no," Donnelly said, wondering if this was the gambit Colby was going to use, separating them.

"Not at all," Pike said.

"What is this about?" Clint asked.

She turned her gray gaze on him fully.

"I thought you and I should have a conversation, Mr. Adams."

"About what?"

She looked at the other two men, and then back at him.

"In private?"

"Of course," Clint said. Donnelly and Pike were both armed, if this was a ploy.

"Are you finished with your pie?" she asked.

He put the last bite into his mouth and said, "I am now." He stood and looked at the other two. "Gentlemen."

"See you in a while," Donnelly said.

As Clint and Ingrid left the dining room, he said, "Where would you like to talk?"

"Someplace private," she said. "How about your room?"

"If you think your reputation can survive that," he pointed out.

She laughed and slid her arm into his.

FORTY

Clint unlocked the door to his room and allowed Ingrid to enter ahead of him. He looked both ways in the hall before following her in.

He closed the door and locked it.

"Beautiful room," she said, turning to face him. "I haven't been in this hotel before."

"Yes," he said, "it's very nice. What can I do for you, Mrs. Colby? Did your husband send you?"

"Oh no," she said, walking around, touching tables and chairs, "he has no idea I'm here."

"Okay."

She continued to roam about the room, touching things—like the bedpost.

"Mrs. Colby?"

She looked at him, as if he'd drawn her out of some reverie.

"Hmm? Oh, please, call me Ingrid."

"Do you think that's wise?"

"Why?" she asked. "Do you think something will happen if we call each other by our first names . . . Clint?"

"I don't think anything will happen," Clint said. "It just may not be . . . proper."

"You'll find I'm not overly concerned with what's proper." She removed her jacket.

Downstairs in the dining room, Pike wanted another slice of pie, so Donnelly joined him.

"What do you think that was about?" Donnelly asked.

"An attempt to split us up maybe?" Pike asked.

Donnelly looked around.

"I don't see any men with guns."

"Did you see them before they started shooting at you last time?"

"No."

"Neither did I." He ate his last chunk of the second piece of rhubarb pie. "Maybe they won't try anything inside the hotel."

"Or at least, not in here or the lobby," Donnelly said. "They might be waiting outside."

Pike looked toward the front windows.

"But what does Ingrid Colby want with Clint?" Donnelly asked.

"Are you aware of his reputation with women?" Pike asked.

"I heard something about—you don't think he'd take a married woman to his room . . . for that?"

Pike stared across the table at Donnelly and said, "You're very young, aren't you?"

Ingrid dropped her jacket on a chair. She was wearing a white silk blouse beneath it.

"It's hot in here," she said.

"I can open a window—"

"Don't bother." She touched the collar of her blouse.

"Ingrid," Clint said, "what do you want?"

"Just to get to know you a little better."

"But we don't know each other at all."

"Well," she said, "we can fix that, can't we?"

Clint was listening for footsteps in the hall. Was she trying to keep him occupied, in preparation for an attack?

"Are you nervous?" she asked. "I thought you had a reputation with the ladies."

"Not nervous," he said, "just aware. You might say . . . suspicious."

"About what?"

"About why a married lady I hardly know would want to come to my room."

"Really?" she asked. "You can't imagine the answer?"

"Ingrid—Mrs. Colby—you're a beautiful woman, there's no doubt, but this . . . this is beneath you."

She reacted as if she had been slapped.

"If you think I can be this easily distracted, you're mistaken."

Her face suffused with blood and she grabbed her jacket off the chair.

"You'll regret treating me this way," she told him.

"Please," he said, "the woman scorned act is even older than the attempted seduction bit. What were you hoping to gain by this?"

"I fear you'll never know the answer to that, *Mr.* Adams," she said, and stormed from the room.

Donnelly and Pike were in the lobby when the lady came charging past them and out the front door.

"Apparently that meeting did not go well," Pike said.

"Let's see what's going on," Donnelly said.

They walked to the door and looked out. Ingrid Colby walked across the street with determined strides and stopped in front of a group of men.

"Uh-oh," Donnelly said.

"Yes," Pike said. "Let's go upstairs."

As Clint let them into his room, Pike said, "She went across the street—"

"I know," he said. "I watched from the window."

"What happened?" Donnelly asked.

"She tried to seduce me."

"And failed?" Pike asked.

"Does that surprise you?"

"Well," Pike said, "Jim West once told me you could find a woman to lie with in a leper colony."

"I'll have to have a talk with Jim about that sometime," Clint said, "but yes, she failed. And I guess she's not used to that. She got kind of upset."

"Upset enough to go across the street to a group of men and . . . what?" Donnelly asked.

"My guess is," Clint said, "she told them to kill me."

Ingrid Colby stormed across the street to where her husband's men were waiting.

"Mrs. Colby—" one of them said.

"Kill them!" she said.

FORTY-ONE

Tom Colby entered the building, his nose assailed by the strong smells of chemicals and ink.

"Sir," one of his two men said.

"How is he, Pete?" he asked.

"Fine."

"Are the two of you keeping him happy?"

The other guard, Ben, looked at his boss and said, "We're letting him have whatever he wants. I don't know if he's happy."

"He kinda wants to go outside," Pete said.

"You haven't let him," Colby said.

"No, sir," Ben assured him.

"Good."

Colby approached the third man in the room, who was bent over some bills, inspecting them with a thick lens. His name was Emanuel Ninger. He had arrived in the United States in 1882 from Germany and—as far as Tom Colby was concerned—the man was an artist. His counterfeit bills were almost undetectable.

Ninger, who was just over forty, looked up from his work as Colby approached.

"I should have remained back East with my family," the man complained. His speech was thick with a German accent.

"Are you unhappy, Herr Ninger?" Colby asked.

"If I wanted to be a prisoner, I could have remained in my own country," the man complained.

"But sir, you are getting everything you want," Colby said. "The finest equipment, the best in inks and paper—"

"I would like some fresh air!"

"Ah, Herr Ninger," Colby said, "that would be much too dangerous for you. Believe me, you are safer right here, doing your work."

"My work is the only thing keeping me sane," Ninger said, and went back to it.

Colby returned to his men.

"Make sure he doesn't go outside."

"Yessir," Pete said.

Colby went outside, where he found Denim and Roburt waiting for him with another man.

"Boss, this is Sergeant Mitchell," Denim said. "He's our inside man."

"What's he doing here?" Colby demanded.

"He's got something important to tell you," Roburt said. He looked at the middle-aged policeman. "Tell him."

"The chief knows about the counterfeiting," the man said. "He's assigned a detective to work with the Secret Service man to find out who's doing it."

"The man who was in the hospital?"

"Yessir. And there's something else."

"What?"

"The detective—his name's Donnelly—he's working with the Gunsmith, too."

"I met both of them last night," Colby said. "They came to my home."

"What for?" Denim asked.

"To ask for my help."

Denim laughed, but stopped when Colby gave him a dirty look.

"Look, Roburt, you and this fella—"

"Sergeant Mitchell," Roburt said.

"Get over to the Mayflower Hotel. You'll find some of our men across the street. Join them and wait."

"For what?"

"Instructions," Colby said, "from my wife."

"From your—"

"Move!"

Roburt jumped, and he and Mitchell scurried away.

"Whataya want me to do, boss?" Denim asked.

"You," Colby said, "go and get me Crane."

FORTY-TWO

Clint watched the men across the street from the window, didn't see anyone he knew.

"Recognize anybody?" he asked Donnelly.

The detective moved to the window, peered out, and then said, "Damn it."

"What?"

"I know one of them."

"Who is he?"

Donnelly looked at Clint.

"His name's Mitchell. He's a sergeant in my department."

"The inside man," Pike said.

"I knew he took money, but this," Donnelly said, shaking his head.

Pike looked out the window.

"Do you think they'll wait, or come in?"

"They'll wait awhile," Clint said, "but if we don't come out, they'll have to come in."

"We could go out the back," Pike said.

"That defeats the purpose of this whole thing," Clint said. "We wanted them to come after us."

"We did," Donnelly said, "but that many? I count . . . seven."

"And we need to keep at least one alive," Pike said. "To point to Colby."

"Only legally," Clint said. "We saw Mrs. Colby walk right up to them. I think it's pretty clear they work for Colby."

"What if it's his wife?" Donnelly asked.

"What?" Pike said.

"What if his wife is behind it all, and Colby doesn't know anything about it?"

Clint and Pike looked at each other, then looked back at the young detective.

"Naaaaaaw," they both said, shaking their heads.

Donnelly shrugged and said, "It was just a thought."

"She's involved," Clint said, "but she's not the one in charge."

"I agree," Pike said.

"So what do we do now?" Donnelly asked.

"We settle down," Clint said, "and we outwait them."

"I'm not used to waiting," Donnelly said.

Pike looked at the young man and said, "You better get used to it."

"Fast," Clint added.

Ingrid Colby slammed the front door of the house as she entered. Tom Colby knew this was not a good sign. He was seated on the sofa as she entered, fuming.

"It didn't go well?"

"I want him dead!" she said.

"He turned you down?"

She glared at him. He let the question go.

"What about the German?" she asked.

"He's hard at work."

"I gave the order," she said.

"Do we have enough men there to carry it out?" Colby asked his lady.

"We should."

"Well," he said, "I have a backup plan in place. It should all be over by morning."

She tore off her jacket and her blouse. Her bare breasts bobbed into sight.

"I want to spend the night fucking," she said.

Colby loved it when she talked like a whore. And he loved treating her like one even more.

"I think that can be arranged," he said, coming up off the sofa.

FORTY-THREE

They decided to douse the light in Clint's room and take turns at the window.

"I'm getting hungry again," Pike said.

"You're healing," Clint said. "But we can't leave the room. Not just yet."

"I also wish I had a bigger gun," Pike added.

"My rifle's in the corner," Clint said. "It's yours to use."

Pike walked to the corner and picked it up.

"This is better."

"Can I have that, then?" Donnelly asked, pointing to the New Line in Pike's belt.

"Sure." Pike handed it over. That actually gave Donnelly two .32-caliber pistols.

"I wish I had something bigger, too," he said, "but at least two guns are better than one."

Clint was at the window at that point, and now he squinted as dusk gave in to nightfall.

"Something's happening," he said.

"What?" Pike asked.

He and Donnelly came to the window.

"They're moving."

"Still seven of them?" Donnelly asked.

"I think so."

"How do we play this?" he asked. "You fellas are more used to shoot-outs than I am."

"That's Clint's bailiwick," Pike said, "not mine."

They both looked toward Clint.

Jack Denim took control.

"Four in the front," he said, "three in the back."

"What if they climb out a window or something?" one of the men asked.

"The Gunsmith ain't gonna run," Denim said. "And the Secret Service man is hurt. You, you, and you are goin' in the front with me. One of you is gonna cover the lobby while the rest of us go upstairs." He pointed to the police sergeant, Mitchell, and said, "You take the other two men to the back door and go up the stairway there."

"We gotta talk," Mitchell said.

Denim took the policeman's arm and pulled him aside.

"What is it?"

"I can't do this, Jack," Mitchell said. "I'm the law."

"You ain't the law right now, Mitchell," Denim said. "You're workin' for Tom Colby, and he's gonna remember what you do tonight when he becomes mayor."

"Jack—"

Denim grabbed the man's arm again, but this time he squeezed hard.

"You better stand up and do this, Mitchell!" he snapped. "This is important."

"Yeah, yeah," Mitchell said, "okay, but . . . I don't wanna be the one to kill Donnelly. I mean . . . he's a police officer."

"Don't worry about that," Denim said. "I'll need most of you to focus on the Gunsmith. I'll take care of Donnelly."

"What about the Secret Service man?"

"He's not gonna be a problem," Denim said. "He's already got holes in him. Now get into position with your men. In five minutes, we're going in."

"Yeah, okay . . ."

Mitchell waved at his two men, and they followed him across the street.

"Get your guns ready," Denim said to his three. "I want you to shoot anybody you see with a gun, get it?"

They nodded that they understood.

Denim drew his own gun as he and his men crossed the street and entered the hotel.

"Okay," Clint said, "they'll be coming in five minutes or so."

"How can you tell that?" Donnelly asked.

"Four of them just went through the front door. The other three ran into the side alley," Clint explained. "They'll be going around back. The timing will have to be right for them all to come in at the same time. We've got at least five minutes to get into position."

"Okay," Donnelly said.

"Pike," Clint said, "you're in here. Just stay put and shoot anybody who comes through that door."

"What if it's you?" Pike asked.

"It won't be me," Clint assured him, "and it won't be Donnelly."

"All right." Pike was used to running investigations, working undercover, but was not very experienced when it came to gunplay.

"And just relax," Clint said. "Don't tense up. Edward, come on," he said, and they went out into the hall.

The same was true of Donnelly. Gunplay had not yet been a big part of his life.

"Go down to the other room and stay there," Clint said. "Don't come out until you hear gunshots."

"Right."

Donnelly started down the hall, then stopped and turned back.

"Clint?"

"Yeah?"

"Can we do this?" he asked. "I mean, there are seven of them."

"We can do this, Edward," Clint said, "but it's a little late to ask that question, don't you think?"

"Yeah," Donnelly said. "I guess you're right." He started away and stopped again. "Hey, wait!"

"What?"

"If Pike's in your room and I'm in the other room," he asked, "where are you gonna be?"

"I'll think of someplace."

FORTY-FOUR

Denim and his men entered the lobby of the hotel. It was dark out, but not late, so there were people there—the desk clerk, some guests, and people going in and out of the dining room. Maybe they should have waited for the dining room to close, but it was too late for that.

"You stay here," Denim said to one of the men. "Don't even draw your weapon unless you see somebody running down those stairs. Understand?"

"Yeah, I got it."

He looked at the other two men and said, "Follow me—and be quiet."

They went up the stairs.

Clint considered waiting for the men in the lobby, but then there were the others who would be coming up the back stairs.

That was when he saw the hatch in the ceiling.

                          * * *

Mitchell and his two men forced open the back door of the
hotel and started climbing the stairs. The sergeant, being
nervous about the whole affair, had moved a few minutes
too soon. He and his men got to the second floor before
Denim and the others.

"What room?" one of his men asked.

Mitchell stopped.

"I don't know," he said. "I can't remember."

"What the hell—" the other man said. "What do we
do now?"

"Fifteen!" Mitchell said. "I just remembered. It's
fifteen."

"Where are the others?" one of the two men asked.

Mitchell, who had been hesitant so far, suddenly grew
impatient and said, "Let's just get this done. There's three
of them and three of us."

"But . . . one of them is the Gunsmith," one man said.

"We better wait for the others," the other said.

Mitchell got nervous again and said, "Right."

Clint was on the roof, listening to the conversation through
the hatch. If he dropped down now, he could kill the three
of them, but what about the other four? Would they come
running up, or be warned off?

Through the opening, he was able to see the door of his
room. He decided to wait.

As Denim and his two men reached the second floor, he
saw Mitchell and his two at the other end.

"What are you waiting for?" Denim called. "Let's go."

They all started down the hall, and Denim stopped in front of room thirteen.

"Oh," Mitchell said, "thirteen!"

As Denim kicked the door in, Clint dropped down through the hatch. He'd considered shooting them from above, but that would be akin to shooting them in the back.

He was no backshooter.

As the door slammed open, Pike levered his rifle and opened fire.

At the sound of the gunshots, Donnelly came running from his room.

The hallway erupted in gunfire.

Denim turned as Clint landed. His eyes went wide and he yelled, "Adams! Get him!"

The others turned to look at Denim, and by the time they realized what was happening, lead slammed into them from all sides.

Pike and Donnelly fired wildly, but their bullets managed to kill three of the men. Clint fired his weapon coolly and killed the other three.

And then it got quiet.

Pike came out of the room, and Donnelly walked down the hall.

Clint inspected the bodies.

"They're all dead."

Donnelly looked at Clint.

"You're shot."

Clint glanced down at himself, saw that a bullet had creased his left shoulder.

"Yeah," he said, "I think one of you did that."

"Jesus!" Pike said.

"Sorry," Donnelly said.

"Forget it." Clint stared down at the dead men. "Couldn't keep one of them alive. Not in that hail of bullets."

Pike counted the bodies and said, "There's only six of them."

"What?" Donnelly said.

"Count 'em yourself," Pike said. "Six." He looked at Clint. "There were seven, right?"

"Yeah. The other one must be covering the lobby."

"Then let's get him," Donnelly said.

He started down the hall, but Clint grabbed his arm.

"We need this one alive," he reminded him.

"Right."

FORTY-FIVE

The seventh man gave up quietly when Donnelly, Clint, and Pike came down the stairs. Once the man had identified Tom Colby as the leader of the counterfeiting operation, Donnelly handed him over to two police officers sent by the chief.

"I hope we can trust those two to keep that man alive," Clint said.

"I know them," Donnelly said. "As far as I can tell, they're honest. And the chief sent them."

"And as far as we can tell, *he's* honest," Clint said.

"So far," Pike said.

They left the hotel and went directly to the Colby house. As they approached the front door, but before knocking, Clint stopped them.

"I'm going around to the back," he said. "Give me five minutes and then knock."

"Right," Donnelly said.

Pike nodded. He was back to carrying Clint's Colt New Line, having left the rifle behind.

"Five minutes," Clint reminded them.

When he got around to the rear of the house, he waited. After three minutes, he forced open the back door. He found himself in the kitchen with Mrs. Preston, the cook.

"Wha—"

He held his finger to his lips, then whispered, "Out."

"You can't—"

"There's going to be gunplay," he said. "Get out."

Her eyes widened. She dried her hands on her apron and slipped out the back door.

Clint moved to the doorway that led to the dining room. He heard some commotion from the other room, was about to go through the door when he heard Colby's voice.

"You can come in, Adams," Colby said. "We've got your two partners covered."

Damn it, he thought. He went through the door, saw Colby and his wife standing there with smug looks on their faces. Pike and Donnelly were off to one side. They had been disarmed, and were standing under the barrel of a gun.

The gun was held by Henry Crane, the gambler.

"You!" Clint said.

"Me," Crane said with a smile. "When you showed up in town, they needed somebody to keep an eye on you."

"He came up behind us," Donnelly said.

"You're a gambler," Clint said.

"Mr. Crane is a lot more than that," Colby said. "He's one of those rarities."

"Rarities?"

"A fast man with a gun who has kept a low profile," Colby said. "No reputation to give him away."

Crane grinned and shrugged. Clint knew he was in trouble. Crane already had his gun out.

"How fast?" he asked.

"Real fast," Colby said. "I've seen him."

"And how much of a gambler are you, Henry? I mean, really?" Clint asked.

"You've seen me play—oh, I see what you mean. Interesting."

"What?" Ingrid Colby asked. "What's interesting?"

"Mr. Adams is proposing a big gamble," Crane said.

"What are you talking about?" Colby asked. "Kill him. And them."

"Do it!" Ingrid shouted.

"Let's not be hasty," Crane said. "This is the Gunsmith we're talking about."

"Henry—"

"A gamble, you say," Crane said to Clint. "You against me."

"If you're really that good."

"Oh no," Colby said, getting it now. "Don't."

"What? What?" Ingrid asked.

"He's going to try him," Colby said. "Henry's going to try the Gunsmith."

"You can't!" Ingrid said. "That'd be gambling with all our lives. You have no right."

That seemed to make the proposition irresistible to Crane.

Colby looked on the floor, where Donnelly's and Pike's guns were.

Crane stepped away from the two men, holstered his gun.

"No!" Ingrid shouted.

"Shut up," Crane said. "Anytime, Clint."

"Big mistake, Henry," Clint said. "This is why you never would have been a good gambler." ·

He drew and fired.

Clint, Donnelly, Pike, and several uniformed policemen they were now sure were honest—since Mitchell, the insider, had been found out—broke down the door of the back room in Tom Colby's farming equipment store.

They found two dead men, and a variety of counterfeiting paraphernalia.

"No German," Donnelly said. "What did you say that fella's name was?"

"Ninger," Pike said. "Emanuel Ninger."

Walking around, Clint stopped at a batch of fifty- and hundred-dollar bills. "He must have killed those two and left the bills behind. Guess he wasn't happy with the working conditions here."

"Yeah," Pike said, "but how many bills did he take with him?"

Clint grinned and said, "That's your job to find out, my friend."

Pike looked at him and grinned back.

"Sure you don't want to come back East with me and find him?" Pike asked.

"Not me," Clint said. "My part ended when I shot Henry Crane."

Pike looked at Donnelly, who shook his head.

"I'm happy here," the detective said.

"Well," Pike said, "I'll transport the Colbys back with

me, and whatever men they have left, get them situated in a nice federal prison, and then start my search for Mr. Ninger."

"You better take some time to heal up first, Pike," Clint advised him. "And for Chrissake, this time get yourself a partner!"

Watch for

THE SOUTH FORK SHOWDOWN

394th novel in the exciting GUNSMITH series
from Jove

Coming in October!